AF266757

Walking a Thin Line

IMOGENE GRANT

Zeta Publishing, Inc
P.O. Box 953
Silver Springs, FL 34489
www.zetapublishing.com

This is a work of fi ction. All of the characters, names, incidents, organizations, and dialogue in this novel are either the products of the author's imagination or are used fi ctitiously.

Ordering Information:
Quantity sales. Special discounts are available on quantity purchases by corporations, associations, and others. For details, contact the publisher at the address above.
Orders by U.S. trade bookstores and wholesalers. Please contact Zeta Publishing: Tel: (352) 694-2553; Fax: (352) 694-1791 or visit www.zetapublishing.com

ISBN: 978-1-950340-12-5 (sc)
ISBN: 978-1-950340-13-2 (e)

Library of Congress: 2019911160
Printed in the United States of America

CHAPTER I

Jonathan and Stephanie snuggled before a warm, crackling fire to share a glass of wine. They had spent a long weekend of skiing, exploring, and reaffirming their love.

They turned to each other on this, their last evening before going home. Nothing existed for them at this moment except each other. He set aside their glasses.

She caressed his face with her fingertips. Their kiss was warm and so sweet. It canied them to the soft white rug before the fire, and desire consumed them. They undressed each other between kisses. The world beyond was as far away as another galaxy.

He kissed her eyes and the soft hollows of her throat. Her hands flowed over his body, exploring, capturing new sensations and building excitement for him as well as herself.

He stroked her firm breasts, first with his hands, then with his tongue. Her face glowed with love in the firelight as she clung to her husband and gave herself to him as fully ,is she knew how.

When the first moments of urgent passion was over, they lay in each other's aims, feeling the warmth from the fire.

This weekend had been one of their happiest times together.

Ski season in Squaw Valley-where the winters are famous for warm days and cool nights, snow play areas, sleigh Lies, snowmobiling, and the apre's-skiing-is unrivaled. The conditions were just right for relaxing.

Mutually they decided without speaking to retire. Jonathan in one swooping motion lifted his wife in his arms and carried her to the bedroom, where he made love to her, this time unhurriedly.

They could not have guessed as they fell asleep that they would never ski another slope or enjoy another cool glass of wine before a glowing fire together again.

They arrived home without fanfare, and they stood in the doorway to the playroom for a moment to watch their son, David, as he sat in the middle of the floor playing a game, while Molly slept nearby. The fact that their children were happy and content made Jonathan's life complete.

David looked up and saw them. He jumped up and ran with outstretched arms, yelling loudly in a child's voice, "Daddy! Mommy! You're home-I didn't know you were here!"

Jonathan scooped his son into his arms and hugged him tightly, tousling his thick dark brown hair. Molly, awakened by the homecoming, began to cry. Stephanie went to her and picked her up, making soothing sounds.

David asked, "Daddy, what did you bring me?"

"Something you'll like. Did you take good care of Molly?"

"I didn't have to; she sleeps all the time. What did you bring me?"

Jonathan walked over and kissed his daughter, slapped his wife on her bottom playfully, and started out of the room. He said to David, "Well, come on. Let's see what we have for you. It was as if the family had never been apart.

Jonathan nestled cozily against his wife; he always felt an excitement when he was near Stephanie. She turned to face him, to be enveloped in a big hug. Stephanie smiled her pleasure, and said, "What's in that very fertile mind of yours?"

"Oh-just watching you."

"Oh, swell, I'm always at my best in the morning," she said with mock sarcasm.

"You look wonderful," he said as he gently pushed a tendril of red hair from her forehead.

They embraced each other with tenderness and mounting passion. She whispered, "I love you-so much." "You are my life," Jonathan said, rubbing his fingertips over her soft cheek. With a kind of reverence he held her close. Her arms encircled his neck as she kissed him hungrily, and together they reaffirmed the beauty of their love. She touched the heavy muscles of his buttocks as his thrusts grew quicker and more forceful, and moaned her pleasure as she felt their intensity grow to a climax.

Later Jonathan, showered and dressed, said, "Come with me to the door." They walked to the front door, arms encircled.

The cab arrived.

Smiling, she said, as she reluctantly released his hand, "I'll miss you."

"This will only take two days. I'll hurry back." They kissed good-bye. She stood on the doorstep and waved good-bye.

She was not a tall woman, barely five feet three. Her long red hair was tied at the nape of her neck. Freckles were scattered across the top of her cheeks and the bridge of her nose. Thirty minutes later he called from the airport.

The telephone rang once. She answered, saying, "Hello."

"Honey, I have a few minutes."

"Yes, sweetheart?"

"I've changed my mind. Ill be home for dinner tomorrow." She allowed herself a smile. Her brown eyes shined warmly as she said, "I'll have all your favorites."

"I have to go now. Arivederci."

"Until then, sweetheart."

"I love you" were his parting words.

Adam Lockhardt had had a *fantastic* morning and a long, four-Martini lunch. He was very drunk when he drove out of the executive garage. His new Rolls Royce purred as he entered the stream of traffic.

As it is with most drunks, he felt omnipotent. His company had two new multimillion-dollar accounts. Today he was in an expansive mood, never realizing he was exceeding the speed limit. He raced along the broad, tree-lined boulevard, through the posh residential area.

Things were going great for him. He had a beautiful wife, a home in Lake View Canyon. His children attended the best schools. These thoughts were in his mind as he ran the stop sign at Casitas Lane and Davenport Road.

The silver-gray Rolls plowed into the white Mercedes, driven by Stephanie Loring. Her four year-old son, David, and his infant sister, Molly, were in the car with her. All were killed instantly.

The heavier car had slammed into the Alercedes with such a force that if those in the latter car had lived, in all probability they would have been human vegetables. Adam Lockhardt lived to walk away.

The wrecked Mercedes and Rolls presented a ghastly sight to an off-duty intern, who quickly determined that the woman and both children were dead and that the driver of the larger automobile had escaped with only minor lacerations.

A second motorist called the police from his mobile telephone. Officers of the highway patrol, sheriffs deputies, and news reporters arrived within minutes, alone with the fire department and medical personnel.

Adam Lockhardt was treated at the scene and taken into custody. Members of the fire rescue squad had to pry the doors to the Mercedes open in order to retrieve its grotesque cargo. The impact bad wedged the smaller automobile between a tree and the Rolls Royce.

When Adam Lockhardt entered police headquarters, his gait was erratic. His speech slurred, he complained that his beautiful car was destroyed, unaware that the mother and children of the other car were killed at the scene.

Lieutenant Miller asked, "What have we here?" The officer replied, "Auto versus auto. Two children and the mother killed outright."

"Any witnesses?"

"Yes." The officer consulted his notebook. "A Mrs.. Sloan saw it all. This guy, Adam Lockhardt, ran the stop sign. Excessive speed. No skid marks to indicate he tried to stop. Plowed right into the Mercedes. The driver of the Mercedes was pulling away from the stop sign."

"Any obstructions? Was there any reason he couldn't have seen her?"

"No obstructions. He is blind drunk." Adam Lockhardt, searching in his pockets and swaying drunkenly, said, "I have money to pay for the car. Don't worry, I'm a rich man. Here, take what you need." He extended his hand, which was filled with hundred of dollars. Everyone around stared at him in disgust.

Miller said, "Put him in the tank, and start processing" He never finished his sentence because Lockhardt chose that moment to vomit all over the desk. The foul-smelling stomach contents splattered the sergeant behind the desk and two officers nearby.

The desk sergeant screamed, "Goddamn son-of-a-hitch Get that bastard out of here.'"

Miller said, "Call someone to clean this up," as he walked away, circling the mess. He asked the officer, "Who are the victims?"

"Stephanie Loring, her son, David, and daughter, Holly. According to her aunt, Mrs. Loring's husband is out of town. A job for his company."

"Has he been notified?"

"Not yet-he's out in the field somewhere. Unable to reach him.."

"The poor bastard. What a way to come home." "Isn't that the way, though?"

"What?"

"The good always die, and we're left with the slime."

"I guess you've got a point," Miller answered as he closed the door to his office.

Jonathan Loring, research engineer, could not be reached for several hours. His assignment: to look over a future project for his company. He was a young man, with good prospects. He had personality, a young family, and a good background.

He was intercepted by Police Detective Gebhardt as he entered the lobby of his hotel. "Mr. Loring? Are you Mr. Jonathan Loring?"

"Yes, I'm Jonathan Loring. What can I do for you?"

"I'm Police Detective Gebhardt." He flashed his badge and identification. "Sir-I'm afraid I have bad news. Jonathan smiled and said, "Are you sure you have the right person? I don't live in this city. What kind of bad news could you have for me?"

"Sir, have a seat over here, please." The detective indicated a couch nearby. Jonathan walked over and sat with a look of growing concern on his face. He said, "All right, I'm sitting. Stop wasting my time and get to the point."

"Mr. Loring, I don't know how to put this, except to say I'm sorry to be the bearer of bad news." With growing impatience, Jonathan said, "Well , get to it. Tell me what's wrong."

"Your family was killed earlier today, in an auto accident."

Jonathan's heart leaped into his throat. He asked, "How? What are you saying?"

"A drunk driver ran a stop sign."

"All dead?" he asked, disbelief in his voice.

"The driver of the other car was unhurt." His expression wavered between shock and disbelief. "My family? Stephanie? David and little Molly? Oh, my God! You *can't* mean they're all dead!"

Gebhardt stood in awkward silence, not knowing what to say.

"My whole family," Jonathan continued, "wiped out - but I just saw them this morning. My wife and I just came home after a long weekend. I'll see them soon. You have the wrong Loring." His eyes begged the detective to say he had the wrong man.

Gebhardt stood by in frustrated silence. He thought that it was a low blow to tell a man his family had been wiped out in only minutes.

Jonathan continued to speak. "This has to be a cruel joke." After a moment's silence, he said, "flow did it hap pen?" He was obviously making an effort to control himself.

"Your wife pulled away after stopping at a Boulevard stop. As her car reached the center of the intersection, the driver of the other car ran the stop sign and hit your wife's car broadside. He was doing more than eighty miles an hour. The driver had been drinking."

Jonathan, as if he had not heard, said, "I have to get to the airport. I have to go home!"

"I'll drive you, Air. Loring."

"What?" he asked, as if he didn't realize the detective ""as still there.

"I said, I would drive you," Gebhardt repeated. "Wait here. I'll get my things."

The grief-stricken man walked to the bank of elevators and pressed the up button. Outwardly Jonathan displayed an icy calm. He fought to control himself. On one side there was disbelief, and on the other there was the hope that the officer had made a terrible mistake.

He entered the sterile viewing room in the city morgue. Three bodies were on the hard slabs. He looked at his wife and children lying there in this cold room. He had not thought it possible. They looked so small. He stood for several moments staring at the mutilated remains of his family. Jonathan struggled with the overwhelming emotions he was feeling as he touched the stiff faces and smoothed the hair of each one. His heart leaped in his chest as the horror dawned on him: they would never run, play, and laugh again.

His face expressed the anguish he felt as he turned to the coroner and asked, "Was it a painful death?"

"No, I'd say death was instantaneous," replied Dr. Gordon.

Jonathan took one last look at his family. How vulnerable they all were. There had been nothing he could have done to help them. He felt so powerless as he struggled against the rage he was feeling. He turned away reluctantly and followed Dr. Gordon into the hall.

Dr. Gordon asked, "Is there anything I can do to help?" Jonathan stalked down the hall toward the outside door and didn't look up or acknowledge the doctor's offer.

Gordon remarked to the morgue attendant, "Air. Jonathan Loring is going to have a very difficult time."

"Yes - he was very upset."

"That's putting it mildly. He is a man trying to control his rage." The doctor paused momentarily and then said, "I wonder just how stable he is."

"That's a bitter pill to swallow, his whole family at once, the attendant answered. "Good point," the doctor said as he opened the door to the office.

When Jonathan emerged from the coroner's office, he seemed more in control. There was still an icy calm about him. He flagged a call and gave the driver his home address. He rode across town preoccupied with his thoughts, and all too 50011 he reached his destination. He paid the driver and walked slowly to the front door and entered.

The reality of the disaster hit him with renewed intensity. He froze momentarily before he slammed his fist into the living-room wall. A low wail escaped his lips. It came from deep down. He was a man whose very soul was in torment. He bad touched that thin line between sanity and insanity.

Funeral services were over.

He felt the emptiness before he was fully awake. He opened his eyes, and then closed them tightly, trying to will reality away.

The silence throughout the house was more than simple absence of sound; it was a void of nothingness.

He climbed out of bed and wandered from room to room, pictures of his family crowding his mind. He remembered corning home from a trip: His wife would meet him at the door, and they would hold each other as though they had been apart for a long period of time. He would squeeze her so tightly she couldn't breathe.

She would say happily, "Jon, I have something special for you," as she would back away, holding his hands and smiling. Then she'd say, "I'm glad you're home; we missed you so much. Have you eaten?"

"No-I waited to have dinner with you."

"Come and sit down. No-go and see David and Molly while I change." She would back away, patting her hair and smoothing her dress. "I love *you*," she'd say.

He would take her gently into his arms and say, "I love *you*." He would caress her face lightly with his fingetips and whisper, "Huny back." Then he would go to see his children.

Molly would gurgle and grin her sweet, toothless arm when he took her from her crib. He'd carry her into David's room and sit on the bed. His son would hop up beside him, grinning and saying, "I'm going to be just like you when I grow up-grow up-" The words echoed in Jonathan's mind. He suddenly remembered there was no future; every-thing was done.

His last day spent in the house that once was his home was spent in memories and following the farce (if the trial for Adam Lockhardt. The ritual was not a trial, but a mockery of justice. His family's killer received a virtual slap on the wrist: one year of probation and useful service to the community. The fine, as well as the sentence, was laughable.

Jonathan stared at the television screen, which showed Lockhardt's grinning face as he emerged from the courtroom. The press was clamoring for his attention.

He listened to the killer of his family as Adam mouthed platitudes and made promises he would only keep until his next drink. The press seemed to hang on each word. Lockhardt was free to kill again.

Jonathan said aloud, "He cannot get away with this. I will not allow it!"

Without forming a conscious decision, he climbed in the car and drove through town to the lake, where he sat on a bench, staring into the water and smoking cigarette after cigarette.

Reality finally caught up with him and engulfed him, like the water that slapped gently against the bank. His wife and children were gone. There was no place to go, no home. He was alone.

Stephanie - her bubbly, bouncy presence-had always cheered him, no matter what problem he had to deal with.

He felt only bitterness and contempt for her killer. He thought, *0 God! Why has it happened?*

There was a heart carved into the bench, with initials on either side of the arrow that pierced it.

He concentrated on the design, trying to blank his mind of the thoughts that welled to the surface.

After a while he walked slowly from the lake and got into his car. Cars flew toward him and passed with a rushing sound as he sat behind the wheel.

Jonathan suddenly remembered he had not eaten, and stopped in a coffee shop nearby and ordered a sandwich and coffee. As he ate slowly and sipped his coffee, he took out a pad and pencil. He planned for revenge. He would have to do some research to determine the means.

There were so many details; this act would require a great deal of careful planning. He stared at the notes he had printed.

   1.   Gun-too noisy-messy Poison
   A. How to select it
   B. How to administer it
   C. How to obtain it
   D. How to store it

He thought as he tapped his pencil on the pad, *I 'will have to explore the details*. When he left the coffee shop and headed for his car, his stride was sure, steady, and relaxed.

He drove to the library in the center of the city. He entered and went directly to the card index; after a few minutes he found the information he needed.

In the stacks he found the book he wanted without difficulty. He sat at one of the tables in the reading room, arranged his pad and pen, and started to read.

Two hours bad gone by. He had a list of four chemical substances, any of which would be suitable to produce the results he desired according to the outline he had formulated during his drive. He walked out of the library and drove in the direction of his former office, a place he would never return to after today. On his way he passed a sign with the legend "The last days are at hand." He read it and thought, *How true*. He arrived at his old office building minutes later.

He entered at the main entrance and crossed the hall to his office. The employees were hard at work; a few of them glanced up and smiled as he passed through the outer office. He went directly to his desk and started to pack, mechanically emptying the desk drawers and the bookshelves of the con-tents accumulated over the last ten years.

June, his former secretary, came in to offer him her best wishes. She said, "I'm so sorry, AIr. Loring. You have my sympathy."

"Thanks, June."

They shook hands and she left the office.

The door to the supply room was midway between the central stairwell and the rear of the corridor. He walked down the hall and opened the door with his key. Some employees entered the room behind him. They passed him and went straight to the back of the room, found the articles they needed, and exited. Then he was alone.

The equipment he needed was stored in a cool comer of the room. He quickly proceeded to take the parts he needed. Then he had arranged everything as he had found it, he took the article he had come for, turned out the lights, and closed and relocked the door.

He stored his belongings in the trunk of his car, and returned to Personnel and relinquished his keys. He felt a sense of accomplishment. A course of action had been devised, and the initial steps had been taken. It was, however, a tentative plan.

He drove within the speed limit, conscious of the sub-stance he carried in his trunk of his car.

The books he had read listed the lethal dosage of each substance. Now he had to devise an effective and foolproof method of administering it.

He went directly to the house to finish packing and to make final arrangement to move.

It was time to go. He stood for several minutes, silently, in their bedroom, breathing the faint but lingering scent of his wife, feeling total emptiness, then cold, blind unreasoning anger. Rage had replaced the values of a month ago.

The simmering anger in recent days had festered in his troubled mind until it had finally burst open to infect and corrode all his old middle-class standards.

He had loved and cherished his wife, the woman who had given birth to their children. His family had all been taken away in seconds-a future destroyed. He was edging over the thin line between sanity and madness.

It took sheer willpower to control the rage he felt at that moment.

A week later he arrived in Glass Cup, Alontana, haunted by his memories. He'd rented a cabin in a remote area nearby, where he would lead a reclusive existence, except for occasional excursions to the country store in town. His weeks were spent exploring the mountains, back trails, and streams. The river was wide, the water clear and free flowing.

It was difficult to believe that only weeks ago he had a family. He could visualize them, and hear the sounds David made at play and see Molly's sweet smile as she'd wiggle and kick when he took her from her crib to cuddle in his arms.

Negotiating the terrain around the mountain became easier with each passing day. Animal life abounded. The river had cut into the earth to create a long gorge. After hiking five arduous miles, Jonathan found that the cliffs became sheer walls. The river at this point rushed on into the far distance.

Jonathan climbed up on a plateau and crossed over the ridge. Suddenly there was a loud clap of thunder, followed by a downpour of rain. He made a dash for a hollow in the hillside fifty yards away, to wait out the storm.

The rain stopped as suddenly as it had started. He left his shelter and continued toward the cabin.

When he was within a mile of the house the thunder began again, as lightning knifed across the sky.

A blinding rain caught him before he reached the small front porch. Two days later he explored the river in the opposite direction, along Butte Point.

He was deep in thought when the mailman materialized out of a grove of trees.

"*Mr. Loring?*"

"Yes, I'm Jonathan Loring."

"I delivered a package to your cabin. set it inside."

"Thanks, I was expecting one."

"Feels like rain. I think I'll try and beat it. Good day. Mr. Loring."

"Good day to you, too," Jonathan said. and he continued on.

He was caught in another light thunderstorm) and narrowly evaded a rockslide. It was still drizzling as he descended from a plateau and crossed the river on a log bridge.

The water roared over the riverbed to unite with inland tributaries that dropped out of the mountains into a valley with grass so green it seemed unreal. The breeze in the valley swayed the trees gently, a breathtakingly beautiful sight.

He thought Stephanie would have liked this place. He decided to camp there for the night. He ordered supplies not stocked by the country store from the city. He chopped wood, hiked for long distances, and did muscle - building exercises that changed the contour of his body. A neatly trimmed mustache and beard altered his appearance considerably.

The townspeople, after overcoming their initial curiosity, left him alone. Their new neighbor roamed the hills alone. He seemed like a harmless young fellow with a lot of misery, probably woman trouble. Quiet fellow., had no desire to be sociable.

On the twenty-first day, Jonathan awakened from a nightmare. He felt desperately alone, abandoned. He needed to do something or to talk to someone. He dressed hurriedly and took a walk along the river, his mind in turmoil. Eventually his thoughts cleared, but the depression and heartrending loneliness remained. By the time he returned to the cabin, he had devised a plan and the method to implement it

Two days later he drove away from Glass Cup.

Aspen, the international ski resort in the Colorado Rockies, offers skiing as good as any in the world. The ski slopes offer a veritable plethora of choices for skiers of all levels. The view of mountain ranges is magnificent from any hill you choose. The lifts open Thanksgiving Day and close at Easter.

Jonathan arrived opening day to mingle with the people and to get in some skiing. He slept restlessly that first night; his dreams had been confused, disjointed. The silence in his hotel room was overwhelming.

He climbed out of bed and dressed for jogging. Lie ran for miles, exerting his mind as well as his body. When he returned, exhausted, he showered, shaved, dressed hurriedly, and went out again. In the restaurant he ordered a large breakfast and a newspaper.

His depressed mood lingered through breakfast. After he had eaten, he opened the paper. The news only served to deepen his dejection. The headlines in the *Aspen Monitor* read:

DRUNK DRIVER KILLS INFANT, INJURES ANOTHER AND TWO SONS

A drunk driver staggered away after his automobile slammed into the car driven by Mrs. Janet Ogilve. She was driving with her two sons and infant daughter when the accident occurred. The impact hurled Mrs. Ogilve and her sons onto a nearby lawn. The distraught mother raced back to the burning car and pulled the dying infant from the wreck. She cradled the infant and pleaded for help, as the other driver staggered away. Winston Helms, the driver of the other car, escaped with minor lacerations and bruises.

In spite of eight drunk driving arrests in the last two years, he had spent only sixty days in jail, and for further offenses he had been handed light sentences.

Mrs. Ogilve and her sons remain hospitalized, in satisfactory condition.

Winston Helms crawled in extreme agony toward the telephone. He struggled to lift the receiver off the hook. The telephone fell to the floor, beside him. He moved as if in slow motion; it was as if his bands had weights attached. His arms and hands were spastic; his fingers did not work properly.

He moved his hand shakily toward the touch-tone dial. Finally he managed to press the button for the operator.

His energy was ebbing fast; it was becoming increasingly difficult to perform the smallest task.

He thought, My *body is failing me*. He could not move. His sight was fading, and gradually the light disappeared, leaving him in total dark-ness.

The operator said, "Operator. May I help you. Operator. May I help you?" He was unable to speak to ask for help. He knew he was dying as he lay there, his mind becoming increasingly detached and surprisingly lucid. He thought of the things he would never do. He remembered something the killer had said as he plunged the needle into his chest. Winston had been helpless from too much bourbon and he had not had the strength to fight. His killer had said, "Stephanie, this is for you." He did not understand that remark.

The excruciating pain took his mind off his killer, forcing him back to the all-enveloping darkness. It was like an enormous wave, sweeping him faster and faster toward the inevitable end: DEATH.

Item-KISG TV News:

The body of Winston Helms was found in his home today. A news article was pinned to his shirt.

Winston Helms, wealthy entrepreneur, was the driver who caused an accident that resulted in the injury of Mrs. Ogilve and her two sons and the death of her infant daughter. Helms had been drinking.

An unnamed source had reported that Mr. Helms had a very high level of alcohol in his bloodstream. In addition, other substances were found, which are as of now unidentified.

It was also reported that the substances plus the alcohol created gross tissue destruction. This seems to have been a *cold, calculated act of murder*.

We will follow this story on the late news. I am Bill Caaning, KISG TV News.

The Hobmi Mansion,a Renaissance-style building created in the mid-twenties by Leland Bedford, industrialist. The dinner party was over, the mansion quiet, as Jonathan entered the study doors. Hobart had passed out on the sofa. He had discarded his dinner jacket and tie, and had started to unbutton his shirt before falling into a drunken sleep.

His killer stood and stared at him momentarily. Rage burned throughout his very being. Hatred of this drooling drunk was all consuming.

Jonathan removed a thin leather case front an inner pocket. Inside the box, in neat, cushioned spaces, were two vials and horizontally aligned at the side, a syringe and two cardiac needles. He assembled the pre-filled syringe and one needle before slapping the sleeping man awake.

Hobart awakened grumpily and asked, "What? What? Who are you?" Nathaniel Hobart stared with mingled fear and disbelief as Jonathan sank the needle into his chest. He said, as he tried to move away, "What have you done?" He stared down at his chest with honor. Jonathan looked at him blandly and answered, "You are going to die."

Hobart tried to respond, but he could no longer speak. A dull film settled over his eyes, and he watched is the objects nearest him faded. He doubled over with agonizing abdominal pain, and as he tried to stand waves of nausea swept over him. Dizziness and confusion overcame him, and he sprayed the expensive carpet with vomit.

He slumped to the floor in progressing unconsciousness. His respiratory rate increased as his pulse rate became slow and irregular. There was a precipitous fall in blood pressure.

Jonathan placed the syringe in its compartment and the case in the inside pocket of his jacket. He turned and left the room the way he had entered.

At the scene of the crime, policemen, technicians, and photographers were all busily looking for clues, fingerprints, or anything that could be used to solve the crime. Inspector Gastelow, of the homicide division of the Aspen Police Department, asked the medical examiner, "What did you find, Doctor?"

"There was a puncture wound through the anterior wall of the chest, into the fifth inter-coastal space. The puncture appears to be made by a large bore needle. The needle tract seems in direct line with the left ventricle of the heart."

Gastelow asked, "What do you think that sweet, sickly smell is?"

The doctor turned his head to sniff the air. He said, "Could be anything. I'll know after the autopsy."

"How soon will you know?"

"I'll get started when I get back to my office." "Are you finished here?"

"Yes, I've gone as far as I can here. I'll have that report on your desk as soon as possible." The medical examiner closed his case and walked away, leaving Gastelow to attend to any loose ends. *Murder number two*, same M.O., he thought.

In another part of town, Jonathan drove to the airport, turned in his rented car, and boarded the ten o'clock flight out of Aspen.

CHAPTER II

Late evening, three years later. The night was clear, moonlit. A slight breeze blew a newspaper gently along the sidewalk. The city was quiet.

A bag lady carried her bundles in an aged shopping cart. Her progress was slow, as she picked through trash cans and searched the gutter and open alleys, collecting bottles, aluminum cans, and anything else she could find. Her straggling, graying blonde hair was pulled into a sloppy bun at the back of her head. Her faded blue eyes were set in a pale, sallow, dirty face. She wore old black shoes, run down at the heels; she wore no stockings to cover the swollen ankles and legs. Her legs were the same sallow color as her dirty face.

She had noticed the car some time ago. The door on the driver's side stood open. When she came abreast of the open door, the tote bag fell from her bony fingers, cans and bottles rolling out and across the sidewalk.

She stood motionless as her eyes adjusted to the dimness inside the car. Her stare turned to horror as it dawned on her that the man inside was dead. He lay half out of the driver's seat.

The quiet of the street seemed to intensify the simple declaration "He's dead'." Then she screamed and screamed. The screeching could be heard for blocks around.

Two police officers on the next street enjoying, the quiet had their evening shattered by the first piercing shrieks. They were the first officers to reach the scene.

They made a systematic check of the death scene. The door to the driver's side was open. The officer shined his flashlight into the dim interior of the car, checking the seats and then the floor. He walked around the car and turned his light on the body.

In death the man's sphincter had relaxed; the corpse had urinated and defecated. The nauseating odor filled the officer's nostrils. He said, "Holy shit." The young policeman spun away from the car and vomited on the pavement.

Headquarters was notified and the machinery was put in motion.

Hugh Miller, a clean-shaven man with a muscular neck and shoulders, recognized the corpse of Det. Timothy Haughton, who had been on suspension for drunk driving. Timothy, had been awaiting investigation into an "Auto vs. Boy Scout incident several weeks ago.

"Sometimes," the lieutenant said to the doctor, who was kneeling beside the corpse, "you wonder just how long the killings can go on. I've seen enough in my life as a policemen to populate a nice-sized city."

Gordon nodded as he stood after examining the body. He was not impressed. There was a strange sweet odor emanating from the corpse, in spite of the odor of excrement. Miller asked, "What was that smell, Doc?"

"It has the odor of acetone or a similar substance. I can't tell until we do some tests."

"How long has he been dead-just off the top of your head?"

"Mmmmmmm." The doctor looked at the lieutenant. "I can't say exactly, but off the top of my head, I'd say two to three hours. Lividly isn't complete, but then the warm weather could have slowed that."

The lieutenant lit a cigarette, inhaled deeply, and looked around the murder scene. He peered into the interior of the car, then moved around the immediate area. He was thirty-six years old. He had been on the force ten years and was generally a very shrewd man. He said, "Come over here a moment, Doc."

The doctor asked, as he walked the short distance between them, "What are you doing here? I never see the heavies of your caliber around these things. As for me, I have to be here."

Why am I here? When the call came into headquarters and the victim was identified as Timothy Haughton - Casey's brother-I had to come. After all, he is, or was, a fellow officer, even though he's on suspension for that mishap several weeks back."

"This could turn into a messy situation, with the Haughton family history on the force and all."

"You finished with the body, Doc?"

"We have all the pictures we need. Yes, I'm done."

"Well," the lieutenant said to the technicians, officers, and ambulance drivers, "let's wrap it up and get this show on the road." He said to the doctor,

"You know, I should have been a doctor. You guys have a soft life-golf on Wednesday, all those pretty nurses." He took the last puff on his cigarette.

"You smoke too much," the doctor said. "In order to solve this thing, I'll have to get back and do some tests."

"What do you think could be the cause of death? Take a guess."

"You got another cigarette?"

"Yeah, here." The lieutenant lit it for him and clicked the lighter closed.

"I can't say- for sure right now, but I can make just a rough guess-and don't hold me to it. That sweetish odor reminds me of a volatile substance in the acetone family. In addition, the victim had apparently been drinking heavily. I can't tell you now how the second substance was introduced, whether by ingestion or injection, but I can say if the substance is in the acetone family, that and alcohol are a lethal combination."

"I can't picture some guy drinking that stuff deliberately."

"Well, now, you see? That's what makes you the top cop and me just your ordinary, golf-playing physician. You get to go out and track this guy down. He'll have his trusty lil' ole bottle of lethal stuff and - voila' - case solved," the doctor said as he climbed into his car.

"All right, already, save it for when we catch the creep'." They left it at that. The doctor rode away after the ambulance.

The lieutenant stood on the scene after the crew had gone, smoking a last cigarette. Finally he looked at his watch, sighing deeply. It was now his unpleasant duty to break the news to Casey, Tim's brother, and his mother, Mrs. Haughton.

Later, one witness, a janitor in a nearby office building, reported that he had seen a tall, well dressed man in the neighborhood. The witness was not able to give a clear description; he could only say that he was Caucasian.

Miller walked through the squad room to Casey's cubicle. He asked, "Can I come in?" Casey looked up and smiled. "Yeah, pull up a seat."

"Casey, I have some bad news, and I won't beat around the bush. Timothy is dead-we think, murdered. His body was found over an hour ago, and I need you to confirm hi; identity. You know the formality."

Surprise and disbelief showed on Casey's face as he asked, "How?"

"He had been drinking, and according to the medical examiner, there is another substance in his circulatory system. They are doing some tests now to find out what that substance is."

Casey stood and said, "Come on, let's get this over with." He grabbed his coat as he walked out the door.

The medical examiner silently led them down the corridor. He opened a small door and pulled the drawer out gently. He folded the sheet back, exposing the corpse's face. Casey nodded his head in configuration. What caused his death?" he asked Dr. Gordon.

"We'll know more after the autopsy, Casey."

"You think Tim was murdered?"

"Yes, I do. There appears to be an anthelmintic that was either ingested or injected into Tim's system."

"How do you know this?"

"Our preliminary testing has shown that much. We will have to do a total autopsy to be sure how it was introduced. We do know the liquid is colorless and volatile; it's toxic to the cellular structure of the liver, kidneys, and heart if taken in excessive amounts. Tim had a massive dose, and along with his alcoholism, it was lethal."

Casey said, "He wouldn't drink the stuff. It had to be murder."

"It looks like homicide, Casey. There's little doubt."

Miller said, "Thanks, Dr. Gordon."

Dr. Gordon walked over to his desk and said as he picked up a strip of paper, "This was pinned to his jacket." He passed the article to Lieutenant Miller. Miller and Casey read it together. It was from the *Herald Guardian* of Friday, April 22, 1982.

BOY SCOUT SERIOUSLY INJURED BY INTOXICATED ON-DUTY POLICEAIAN

A police officer was found guilty of driving while under the influence of alcohol. He had a blood alcohol level of .25.

Despite prior suspensions, Police Sergeant Timothy Winslow Haughton was given a virtual slap on the wrist today by Judge Deerbome.

The sergeant has been suspended from active duty pending investigation.

Sergeant Haughton, while on duty earlier this month, drove his car wrecklessly into a playground and pinned Paul Kinsington, a boy scout, against a wire-mesh fence. The sergeant had been assigned at that time to desk duty for former drunk-driving charges.

The driver pleaded no contest to driving while under the influence of alcohol.

Judge Deerborne gave Officer Haughton a suspended 90-day sentence and a $500 fine. His license was revoked.

Paul Kensington, the boy scout, is in critical condition at Holy Cross Hospital. The twelve-year old boy scout is not expected to walk again. He is paralyzed from the waist down.

Mrs. Haughton, a large woman with a voluptuous figure for her age, burst into Miller's office. with the air of authority, she said, "Have you found my son's killer?" Miller looked up with surprise. "No, but we're working on it. He paused and then said, "Won't you be seated?"

"Why aren't you out trying to find the killer?" She sat across from him in the visitor's chair. "We are doing our best, ma'am. It's police procedure, we-She rudely interrupted. "My son had enemies. The child he ran into-that awful accident. "What about the family? The father said he would get even.

"We are checking that out now, Airs. Hauoghton," he said as he lit a cigarette from the previous butt.

"Lieutenant, if I may say so' you smoke too much," she said as she eyed the overflowing ashtray.

"I'm aware of that, ma'am. Does the smoke bother you?"

She continued as if she hadn't heard him. "Of course, I didn't approve of Timothy's drinking. What decent Godfearing mother would?"

This was not a question to answer. "The fact remains, Timothy was my' son, ' she continued, "and he was murdered. You are aware of that, I'm sure?" He nodded yes; his cigarette smoldered in the full ashtray.

"I don't see any great effort being made around here to find the killer. You all appear so apathetic. What is being done-aside from sitting here smoking one cigarette after another?"

"The investigation is in progress, I can assure you.

She interrupted, "I have never been told the circumstances surrounding my son's death. How did he die? I have a right to know'."

"Hearing the details,"-he crushed out the smoldering cigarette butts and emptied the ashtray- "what purpose would it serve?"

"Don't give me the runaround, young man!"

"The fact is, he's dead, and death is final."

Very well, you won't tell me?" She stood and said, "I will go now, but you will be hearing from me.

"Ill have someone take-"

"Don't bother, I'll manage, she said as she stalked out the door.

He slumped behind his desk and thought momentarily about lighting another cigarette. He muttered, "You do smoke too much." He searched through the papers on his desk until he found the autopsy report. He picked up the phone, dialed, and waited for someone to answer. Then he said, "Doc, Hugh Miller."

"How are you?" Dr. Gordon answered.

"Never mind that. Listen, can I run down and go over this report with you?"

"Yes, come on down." He hung up the receiver, picked up the report, and slammed the door on his way out.

Minutes later, Lieutenant Miller opened the door to Dr. Gordon's office, tossed the autopsy report on his desk, and said, "Please explain this to me, in English."

"First of all, the victim was drunk and apparently sleeping it off when along comes our friendly killer, who gives him a booster shot."

"Don't get cute. What kind of booster shot?"

"Okay, Hugh. This killer seems to have some knowledge of chemistry and a good knowledge of plants and their properties. He has concocted an extract of the *Nerium oleander* using an industrial solvent."

"I've heard of solvents, but I thought it was used as a cleaner. And what's *Nerium oleander?*"

"The solvent or cleaner is used mainly for industrial purposes. He paused. "*Nerium oleander* is a poisonous evergreen, a shrub, whose roots, flowers, seeds, and bark contain a cardiac glycoside. Said plant's properties have a characteristic action on the heart."

"What does it do?"

"It increases the force of the heati's contractions and acts as a conduction-system depressant. It decreases the cardiac rate. It also has a corrosive effect on cardiac cells and other tissue. This, in addition to the solvent used to prepare the extract, causes damage to all tissue cells." He stopped and then continued. "Hugh, we found a helluva lot of tissue damage to all systems. There's no doubt about it-he wanted to make sure Tim died." He shuddered and continued. "I have never seen such destruction. This concoction is a concentrated preparation of a vegetable drug, obtained by removing the active constituent from the plant. This is done with a suit-able solvent. In this case an industrial cleaner was used in a more modest amount. You have to get this guy. He is a cold-blooded killer, and probably as mad as the proverbial hatter."

"Is that all you found?"

"No, this particular victim had cardiac tamponade."

Exasperated, Miller said, "Okay, you got me. What's a tamponade?"

"Thought you'd never ask. It's an accumulation of fluid and/or blood in the pericardium, the sac surrounding the heart. In this case, the extract would have done the job, but the tamponade was an enhancement."

"You do love your job. How did it happen? What caused the tamponade?"

"On close examination, we found a needle tract. The extract was injected through the aereolar tissue of the breast into the cardiac muscle. The killer probably used a large-bore cardiac needle."

"Okay, is that all?"

"Well, isn't that enough? What do you want me to do, go out and find him?" Dr. Gordon said, smiling a toothy grin.

"Why not." Miller said as he opened the door to leave. "Then I could improve my golf game." Then with a seriousness in his voice, he said,

"Thanks, Doc."

"Don't mention it. Glad to help. Oh, Hugh, one other thing: this extract is lethal stuff for drinkers, especially if there is liver damage already', which is true of l l l(lSt alcoholics and serious drinkers."

Miller stepped back into the room. "Go on, Doc. I know there's something else on your mind." "This solvent can be found 'in an unlimited supply in any public building with this type of fire extinguisher. It's a nonflammable solvent and cleaner in factories garages, and household floor waxes and cleaners. - fatal dose is three to five milliliters. This guy injected a massive amount directly into the cardiac space. The heart had to have pumped it into the system, because of the widespread damage to the cellular structure throughout the body-the central nervous system, kidneys, blood vessels, and liver."

"My Lord, that's so extensive, it boggles the mind."

"I can't say it more forcefully. The ethanol ingestion increases the effect of solvent on all organs, especially the liver-"

"Uh huh, go on."

"The plant extract increases the heart's contractile force, pushing the substance, so to speak, throughout the body." He paused. "Hugh, you've got to get him. He's intelligent and has the means and the know how ....Okay, now I'm finished."

"Well, no golf after all, I guess."

Dr. Gordon smiled and waved him out the door.

CHAPTER III

It was 2:00 A.M. Jonathan followed the Maserati as it raced along the curving ribbon of highway.

The man in the car ahead was unaware of being followed. He didn't feel the slight earthquake as he drove into the grounds of the estate. He was not aware of the shaking as he stepped out of the car. He stood tall, trying,, to get his balance in order to walk a straight line to his front door. He did not know or care how much he had had to drink. He was a big man, over six feet tall, whose muscles had begun to tum to flab. There were remnants of his good looks, although in recent years they were fading.

When he reached the front door after maneuvering the broad steps, he tried to focus his eyes on the keyhole. He dropped his keys twice before finally managing to unlock the door.

He entered the broad front hall with the unsteady gait of an extremely drunk man. He did not bother closing the front door, as he staggered to the circular stairs. He stumbled on the first riser, staggered backward a few steps then made a running start to the stairs again. This time he tripped on the bottom step. He lay' where he had fallen. and said out loud, "Fuck it," and immediately fell asleep. He never awakened again.

Jonathan stared at the man. In that instant his hatred of that drunken sot was overwhelming. His cold, blinding rage toward the man lying there knew no bounds.

He removed the smooth leather case nestled in an inner pocket of his coat. There, in their individual compartments, were the pre-filled syringe and two cardiac needles. His lips slowly formed a smile. One could always depend on the drunks to be obliging. They always passed out. He took his time and attached the needle to the syringe. His smile turned into a grimace as he plunged the needle into John Wick's chest. The sweet odor was perceptible as he removed the needle, and a droplet of blood oozed from the puncture site.

He retraced his steps to the white Mercedes, which was parked in the circular driveway, near the Maserati. The neighborhood was quiet because the homes in the area were far apart. He climbed into his car and drove into the street.

While officers and technicians searched throughout the home and surrounding lawn and driveway looking for clues, reporters created a mob scene outside the gates of the estate. The family and servants had been questioned and released.

Hugh Miller, with the inevitable cigarette, and the medical examiner watched as the ambulance attendants placed the body on the stretcher and shoved it into the dark recesses of the county hearse. An attendant jogged over to them. He asked, "Will that be all, Dr. Gordon?"

"Yes, that's all, thanks. Leave him in the cold room. I'll take care of him when I get there later."

The man nodded and went back to the hearse. The doctor closed his bag with a snap. "No golf for you today, either." He said.

The lieutenant stared down at the article that had been attached to the body. The same sickly sweet odor permeated the still air. He said, "Yeah, I suppose," and then looked up and said, "Well, what do you think, the same M.O.?"

"Yes, it looks right now like the same concoction."

Miller said get this, Doc." He read from the article he held" John Wicks, executive vice president of Strabol Industries, involved in drunken brawl. Two critically injured persons are being treated at Alen-itt Hospital.

'Two blocks later, he sideswiped six parked automobiles and plowed through the plate-glass window of a well-known restaurant. The police, minutes later, removed him from his car, where he had slumped over the steering wheel, unconscious.

'He went before Judge Deerborne and was released on his own recognizance the next day.'

He paused after reading the article and then said, How do you like that? An engraved invitation to murder."

Dr. Cordon said with vehemence, "Good Lord, Hugh, this thing scares me. This is worse than guns any day. You figure it's the same guy did this?"

"Possibly-how the hell would I know? There are no clues. The front door was wide open when his wife arrived home at three-thirty this morning. She said they had had a fight at some gathering, and he left her there. He was obviously noted for his drunkenness and brawling."

"Hugh, I've done all I can here. I'll see you downtown."

"Okay, Doc. See you later."

The doctor picked up his medical bag and walked away. The lieutenant turned to the uniformed officers and technicians and asked, "You guys got all you need?" They all nodded affirmatively. He said, "All right, let's wrap it up." He lit another cigarette before he climbed into his car.

Det. Sidney Brown was a tall, muscular man with a fetish for being neatly dressed. His suits ranged in color between dark blue, brown, and charcoal gray. Lie always wore white shirts and the appropriate tie. The city was his territory. He was raised on the South Side, and except for a stint in the armed services, he never left. For him, the city was alive. He was attuned to it and its pulsating and changing rhythms. He and Raymond Gonzalez entered Lieutenant Miller's office to make their report. They were quite a pair.

Raymond, like Sidney, "as always well groomed. Lie had the physique of a bullfighter in his prime. He had been brought up in the Barrio, and was quiet and introspective. He had learned patience from his enemies; indeed he was an easygoing man who believed that "patience is a rewarding virtue." He had dark brown, intelligent eyes and locks of thick black hair.

They both spoke. "Good morning, Lieutenant." Miller returned the greeting with a nod. Sidney began. "We checked the computer and hit the jackpot. The murders started over thirty-one months ago, in Aspen, Colorado. Their replies are being sent to us. They cover four states so far. We're still checking."

"The same M.O. each time?" Miller asked incredulously.

Raymond spoke for the first time, in his soft, accented voice. He said, "Yes-there seems to be a pattern forming. The killings so far have revolved around a season or special event."

"What do you mean?"

"Murder number one took place in Aspen, Colorado, after Thanksgiving, when ski season began three years ago. "Number two took place in Monterey during the Cocours d' Ele'gance, or the rally for vintage cars. Number three, in Carmel during the Bach Festival, held in July in Sunset Center. The festival brings some of the world's finest Musicians to Monterey."

Miller said, '"Raymond, follow this lead and see where it goes here in the city. Anything more?" He looked from one man to the other.

Sidney replied, "All coroner's repotis coincide with Doe Gordon's - the same needle track, same substance, although the needle track is not necessarily into the cardiac space.

"You're kidding?" Miller said as he lit a cigarette and inhaled deeply.

"No, two victims had punctures into the cerebellum, the base of the brain, which caused massive cellular damage to the brain tissue."

"Well, I can say one thing for the bastard: he really in-tends to kill his victims were news clippings found on all the bodies?"

Raymond replied, "Yes, same M.O. right down the line-except that one variation, the solution being injected into the brain."

"So far no clues to his identity?"

"None at this time," Sidney said.

"You've done some good work. Keep me posted on any new developments, and on your way out send Lampley in."

Thomas Lampley, fifty years old, always seemed to sweat, even in winter. He was an overweight man who had a slight wheeze when he breathed. He never ran or climbed stairs unless absolutely necessary. Lie was also one of the most experienced and meticulous detectives on the force. He entered Miller's office after two knocks.

"You wanted to see me, Lieutenant?" Lampley asked.

"Yes. I've got Raymond working in the city on these killings. I want you to check them from another angle. Check with all cities where the other murders took place. Talk with the officers involved in the initial investigations. Look over the areas where the victims were murdered, questions employees, residents-" He thought for a few seconds and continued. "Check to see if there was a person or group of people new at these special events, any newcomers. Thomas, take your time, and don't leave a stone unturned or clue unchecked, no matter how remote the possibility."

"Okay, Lieutenant. I'll get right on it." He turned and left the office.

Wlson Aymes staggered along Lake Tyre Trail and fell into the path of a late afternoon jogger. He whispered, you have to stop him!" The victim tried to point toward the playground area, and said, "He-he's the-" He stopped and swallowed. "The killer is-" was his last effort before he died, lying in the path of the bewildered and speechless jogger.

The murdered man's shivering gave way to paroxysmal twitching of his hands, arms, shoulders, and neck as a grand mal seizure consumed his entire body. Blood dribbled from the corner of his mouth as his teeth sank into his tongue. Over-head, the lights faded into total blackness. He knew he was dying and fought the sensation feebly. As he died his mind cried out, It *can't happen like this. I have so much to do - It can't-*

The horrified jogger stared at the dead man helplessly. Moments later, he said, in a croaking voice, "Call the police someone! This man needs help!"

A strip of paper attached to the dead man's jacket fluttered in the gentle breeze. One of the bystanders stopped a cruising squad car.

The jogger told the policeman, "I saw him staggering along the path. I thought he was just another drunk, and he just fell at my feet."

"Did he say anything?"

"He tried to point to his killer. The playground over there." He pointed in that direction. "But he died before he could tell me anything. This news article fell out of his shirt pocket."

The next day the following article appeared:

A MURDERED MAN STAGGERS INTO PATH GF JOGGER

A dying man staggered and fell into the path of Ernest Nelson as he jogged around Lake Tyre Thursday evening. Mr. Nelson states, "The victim tried to identify his killer, but died before he could name him."

The coroner's report indicates the same lethal dose of extract that killed twenty other victims in four states. In each case the victims were injected with a massive dose of the concoction. The killings have been labeled the "Extract Murders."

Hugh Miller. after reading,, the morning news, exclaimed, "Damn. How did he get that bit of information?" He grabbed the telephone and dialed. He said, when the receiver was picked up on the other end, "Doc, did you see the morning papers yet?"

"No, I haven't had my coffee yet. either. Why?"

"We've got a leak somewhere. It's all over the newspaper and probably on television about the 'Extract A Murders.'

"The hell you say'." the doctor said incredulously. "How did he find out?

"I don't know, Hugh. No one here would leak it."

"Will you double check?"

"Sure, Hugh"

"Thanks, Doe. Ifl find him, he'll lie pounding a beat out in the toolies." The captain of the department called Miller at 9:00 a.m.

Lieutenant Miller cradled the telephone between his cheek and shoulder to hold it in place as he opened a pack of cigarettes. He said, "Yes, Captain. No, I-" He paused to listen and light a cigarette, then said, "No leads at all. No witnesses to the actual crimes, only the jogger, who said that the last victim fell into the path. He didn't see the actual killing or the killer."

"Where did the papers get the autopsy Teport? You have read the papers this morning?" His voice was loaded with sarcasm.

"Yes, I've read the-" Miller said and listened for a short period.

"We can't have any more leaks to the press. I want them plugged on your end".

"I know, we're working on that now. I've checked with Dr. Gordon. He says there were no leaks from his staff. though they had to get the information from the autopsy report."

"That kind of reporting I could attribute to the *Times Guardian*. They're a slick bunch; you have to be careful."

"I will."

"Did the report label the killings the 'Extract Murders'?"

"No, it didn't. The *Times* reporter probably thought it was a phrase that would catch on".

"Well, he was right. This kind of reporting can make the police look bad. So watch it in the future."

"I can assure you we'll be very careful from now

"I want all the manpower you can spare working on this. Work around the clock if necessary to catch this creep."

"Yes, sir. Good-bye, sir," Miller said. He placed the receiver down gently and said aloud, "Work around the clock? He must be out of his Goddamn mind'."

Later, the detectives were assembled in Miller's office.

"I trust you've read the news today," Miller said. Everybody nodded in affirmation of having read the news. had a leak somewhere in our lines of communication. The killings have been labeled the 'Extract Murders. '" He paused for a moment and then said, "I was on the telephone a while ago talking to the captain, and his instructions were to plug the leaks and work around the clock to get the creep doing the killings."

Sidney Brown asked, "What clock did he have in mind? I've got news for him: We've already worked twenty hours a day on this. Besides, tomorrow is my day off."

"I know, and you will get it unless we have a disaster".

Raymond Gonzalez then asked, "What do we know about this killer? Has a profile been done?" "Yes, I've spoken with the shrink and he says that in all probability, our man had a tragedy caused by an alcoholic and that he would probably appear normal to you or me.

"A witness in Tim's murder case saw a tall, slender, well-dressed Caucasian man in the vicinity. His features were not distinguishable, and he is probably in his mid- to late thirties."

"Not much to go on," said Brown.

"I'll agree with that," Gonzalez said.

Miller said, "You men hit the streets, and, as the saying goes, 'Leave no stone unturned. '" Miller turned to Gonzalez. "Check the computer. List the death caused by drunks-get someone to help you."

He waited until the door closed, and then read through the news clippings again. Editorial: David Straub's Column

A new kind of avenger stalks the streets, one with a knowledge of chemistry and the ability to use it. He is wreaking havoc with alcoholics and heavy drinkers.

The victims were all struck down while under the influence of alcohol, and in varying stages of inebriation. Emanating from each victim was a sweetish odor.

"The killer apparently' has some knowledge of anatomy', because he has found the heart as accurately as any' physician," said an expert, who would rather remain anonymous.

Lieutenant Hugh Miller is in charge of the investigation in this area. Alcoholics, beware. A new type of vigilante is out there.

Miller moved the clippings over to one side and picked up the autopsy report and read it again. He placed it on top of the clippings. Last he read Lampley's report collected froiii other cities. Lampley wrote:

A. All autopsy reports coincide.

B. Interviews with groundskeepers at Lake Tyre they all agree, no one saw or heard anything.

I. There were several people in the park in addition to the regular joggers.

2. Strolling amorous young couple.

3. An older couple-more observant-saw a tall, slender, well-dressed man, too well dressed for a stroll in the park.

Afterthought:

It was believed that the man had a well-groomed mustache and neatly trimmed beard.

4. Bill Deereman, from a nearby apartment complex, said while walking two poodles, he met the man, but did not take notes of his looks and could not identify him. But he did remember that the man was Caucasian.

5. Two young men tossing a Frisbee around were too busy to notice.

6. One groundskeeper remembered that a tall, well-dressed man walked toward the west gate. He did have a mustache and beard.

7. Big black guy sat on a bench near the lake feeding the pigeons for some time. (Police unable to locate black man.) When the dying man fell into the path, there was some excitement before the police arrived, and the black man disappeared.

8. Another groundskeeper noticed a well-dressed man walk back along the path, have a drink from the fountain, then walk on throtigh and out the park in an easterly direction.

Miller circled the statements describing the man with the mustache and beard. A germ of an idea started to form in the back of his mind, an elusive wisp of knowledge he couldn't quite grasp. He blinked and massaged his eyes, and lit a cigarette. Then he looked at his watch and was surprised that it had been almost two hours. lie locked the clippings and reports away. His eyes ached, and he had smoked too much, as usual. He emptied the overflowing ashtray, placed his burning cigarette in it, shrugged into his coat, and made sure everything was in order. Then he picked up his cigarette, took a drag, inhaled deeply, and said with disgust, "I do smoke too much," as he crushed the butt to shreds and left the office, slamming the door.

CHAPTER IV

The judge's gavel sounded loudly.

With disgust, Jonathan whirled and headed for the courtroom door. He thundered down the stairs and out onto the sidewalk. He looked around for a minute, not really seeing the passerby. It did not seem fair that these killers could get by without punishment.

He noticed a stationery store nearby. Within minutes he had written a note in bold block letters to Judge Deer-borne; he felt a sense of satisfaction. He would give him forty-eight hours before he'd do something on his own. He really had no choice.

Apparently a vital thread that linked him to reality had snapped. He had gone for long periods of time without eating or sleeping, brooding for hours.

A passerby would have thought, looking at the calm facade, that he'd be capable of dealing in a rational way with any situation. Yet his inner turmoil was far from reassuring,.

Neva Stephens's last dinner guest had departed. Her heels clicked angrily as she walked through the broad hall. She pushed open the door to the study. Her husband lay before a very expensive painting. His chest was heaving violently; his face was a bluish color.

Neva rushed to his side and knelt down. With fear in her voice, she asked anxiously, "What's wrong?"

His eyes fluttered open and rolled up in the sockets. "Help!" Neva yelled as she ran into the hall. "Help'."

The housekeeper and cook came running from the back of the mansion; the butler entered the hall from the dining room. The housekeeper, after assessing the situation, dialed the paramedics.

The first paramedic could feel a rapid, thready pulse, and lie said, "Feels like tachycardia. Better get the monitor set tip; we'll need a strip." The second paramedic ripped the patient's shirt open to apply the electrodes. The first technician wrapped the blood-pressure cuff around the patient's arm. He pumped the cuff up with air and said, "Forty ,over zero. Heart rate too fast to count."

Neva sat miserably on the couch, afraid to move.

The first paramedic asked, "Any history of cardiac problems, Mrs. Stephens?"

She looked at him and said, "No, he doesn't have a cardiac history." She began to sob. The first paramedic contacted the hospital. "Base II to Base I."

"Base I. Dr. Edmonds, over."

"Dr. Edmonds, we have a male Caucasian, approximately forty-nine years old. B/P forty over zero. Pulse: thready. No history of cardiac problems. Stand by for a strip."

Dr. Edmonds responded, "Ventricular tachycardia. Give a bolus of lidocaine one ampule. Start an IV 500 milliliters of five percent dextrose and water. Keep one ampule of atropine nearby in the event he goes into bradycardia."

The second paramedic injected the bolus of lidocaine.

Dr. Edmonds shouted into the receiver, "His pattern is deteriorating. What happened?" The first paramedic said, "No palpable pulse. unable to get a blood pressure.

Dr. Edmonds, "Give one ampule atropine now!"

"Atropine-one ampule, given."

"His pattern continues to deteriorate. We have an agonal rhythm.. Give one ampule epinephrine and cardiovert."

"One ampule epinephrine given."

"No better. Cardiovert now!" Dr. Edmonds shouted !

The first paramedic applied the cream to the monitor paddles. The second paramedic said, "Four hundred Watts per second."

The first paramedic placed one paddle on the victim's chest directly above the heart, and the second laterally to the left chest wall. He said, "All right, stand back." He pressed a button and in seconds the patient's body contracted and jumped off the floor.

Dr. Edmonds instructed, "Start CPR. We have straight line. Give sodium bicarbonate, one amptile. followed with one ampule epinephrine.

Both were given, without results. The paramedics working hurriedly against time. Dr. Edmonds shouted, Carduivert!"

The second paramedic set the machine while the other applied the cream and placed the paddles. The second paramedic said, "Four hundred watts per second."

"Clear!" the first paramedic, shouted.

Dr. Edmonds said, "Gentlemen, your patient has expired. Pack it up there and transport."

The mayor listened with unconcealed anger to the 6:00 A.M. newscast.

A string of murders across four states has made the headlines in recent weeks. The killer struck again last night. Another victim was added to the serial-type murder list. The body of a 49-year-old real estate entrepreneur was found late Thursday evening by his wife. He was said to be lying on the floor of his study. He died in spite of the efforts by paramedics.

A sweet odor permeated the room. The victim was identified as Alexander Stephens. The investigating officer said they had no suspects and no motive for the killings. Air. Stephens had recently completed a multi million dollar merger with Lands Incorporated.

He had spent the evening celebrating with friends. The victim was a reported heavy drinker, and had gone to his study to lie down and sleep it off.

There was the inevitable news item attached to his shirt. He had been involved several weeks ago in a drunken brawl in a restaurant and had later kicked a miniature poodle to death.

Mrs. Stephens found her husband after the dinner guests had departed. The announcer paused and then said, "We will return after this message for sports and weather."

His Honor, Mayor Bradford, a distinguished politician and gracious host, exuded elegance as he turned the radio off after hearing the news of the latest murder.

His rage was awesome when he telephoned the police commissioner that morning,,. He waited impatiently while the telephone rang. The police commissioner answered sleepily. He said, "Hello."

The mayor said loudly into the mouthpiece, "This is Mayor Bradford." Then he yelled, "What kind of Goddamn police force are you running, where some of the most influential people are being murdered all over the place. What the hell are you doing,, about it!"

The commissioner said. "Well-"

Rudely, the mayor continued, "I would also like to know why there isn't adequate police protection! Can you tell me why!"

"Sir," the police commissioner began again.

The mayor yelled into the speaker. "I want results!"

The police commissioner said, "Yes, sir. We're doing,, the best we can with the equipment and men we have to work with."

The mayor yelled, "You'd better do something and do it soon or I'll have your ass on a platter! He slammed the receiver down..

Huntley B. Beaderman mumbled, "Son-of-a-bitch has the IQ of a rock," as he dialed police headquarters.

Lieutenant Miller had his own headache this morning with the recent murder. He had come up through the ranks and the police commissioner had been appointed two years earlier. The lieutenant had been outspoken on many occasions about the commissioner of police and his blatant political ambitions.

He answered the phone that morning on the second ring and said, "Central Division. Lieutenant Miller speaking."

Without preamble the caller responded, "This is the police commissioner speaking. What the hell is going on down there, Miller?" There was a tremor in his voice. "I'm catching hell from the mayor and everybody else. What are you doing about those killings?"

Miller answered, "We are doing all we can to catch him, sir.

The commissioner shouted, "Well, it isn't enough.. I-want-results!"

Miller cut in rudely saying, "Cut out the bullshit, Coin-missioner, and get us some help down here. We have 'limited' men and equipment."

The commissioner, now calmer, said, "Get some from the City. I'll clear the way." He continued, "I want you to get some men into that area and find that *bastard* before he murders everybody in the damn city. What's this I hear about similar murders in four states?"

Miller, through gritted teeth, said, "It's trne about the murders in four states. We'll do our best, sir. The commissioner, his voice rising, said, "And report back to me."

Miller ended the exchange by saying, "Yes, I will, Sir" He replaced the receiver and said to no one in particular, "That bastard has the balls of a gnat. He wants 'results'!

"That's all I needed. The son-of-a-bitch has made my damn day." He stormed out of his office to a near-empty squad room. Stampley was standing near his desk, chatting with three uniformed officers.

Miller shouted, "Where the hell is everybody? What am I running here-a damn result?"

Stampley and the officers were surprised at the outburst. Stampley said, "Leaves were cancelled last night. All available men are out now rechecking the evidence. Sidney could not be reached."

Miller grabbed the telephone and began dialing. The phone rang loudly in Sidney's apartment. He answered sleepily, "Hello."

Miller's voice exploded into his ear. "Why aren't you here?"

Sidney Brown answered, "This is my day off. Don't you remember?"

Miller said peevishly, "All leaves, vacations, and days off were canceled before midnight. So get over here-on the double!"

Sidney, more awake now, asked, "What's up?"

Miller answered, "Another murder. Meeting,, in my office in one hour." He slammed the receiver down.

Sidney stared at the instrument before replacing the receiver on its hook.

Jinx, his wife, sat up, rolled out of bed, and shrugged into her robe. She asked, "What's wrong, honey?" Her soft, curly hair was like a crown on her shapely head. She was a long-legged, green-eyed, golden beauty, with full breasts and wide hips that tapered into a tiny waist.

Sidney answered, "Another murder; no more leaves for a while." He playfully slapped her on her shapely den-iere as he started for the bathroom to shower and shave.

Later, Sidney and Jinx stood near the door. He thoroughly kissed his bride of two weeks. Looking at her lovingly, he started out the door and said, "If you gotta go, you gotta go.

She said, "Take care, honey."

Captain Winters was well groomed, and this set him apart from some of his observing Contemporaries. His steady gaze was not intimidated by the stares he was receiving as he studied the participants before he spoke.

He said, "Lieutenant Miller has done extensive work on the so-called 'Extract Murders.' He is here to bring you up to date on his progress so far." He turned to Miller and said "Lieutenant Miller."

Miller stood, looked over the detectives and technicians all gathered for a common goal, and slowly began to speak. "In the past six weeks we have uncovered seventy-five killings that have a similar MO. The murders have been spread over four states. Our computer checks have revealed seventy-five to date. We are still searching; there could be more.

"We do not have a clue as to who the killer is, although it's obvious he is killing affluent alcoholics and heavy drinkers, quite possibly due to some past grudge.

"The extract is fast acting. It seems to immobilize the victims within a very short period after the injection. It causes seizures and total cellular destruction throughout all the body's systems.

"We know he is arrogant - to the point of writing the judge in a few cases. He also leaves a calling card of sorts: a news clipping of the victim's past transgressions.

"I have here a letter from Judge Peter Deerbome, of the Nineteenth District Court. 'Lieutenant Hugh Miller: Enclosed you will find two letters addressed to me. They are supposedly concerning the alcoholics that appeared before me. Judge Deerborne.'

"Letter number one. 'Saturday. Judge Deerbome: I use the term loosely because you have ceased deserving the title of "Judge."

"'I see in today's paper that an alcoholic was released by you with a minor slap on the wrist for drunk driving and subsequently crippling an innocent child.

'You will find said DRUNKARD in his car in the garage, at 1 1300 Tucker Drive. I have corrected the bungle you made by releasing this animal.

'In the future any drunks you set free to cause death and destruction will be eliminated in the same manner. Out-raged..

"Letter number two 'Wednesday. Judge Deerborne:

You will never learn. The animal you released can be found in his automobile at 1711 Wilshire Blvd. Outraged.'

"The deaths have been especially vicious. I think it safe to assume the killer has a grudge against people who overindulge in alcohol. In addition, the victims are affluent. Obviously there is a connection between this group and the killings.

"The murderer is educated and has some knowledge of chemistry. He has developed an especially' fast-acting and deadly extract that does irreversible damage. I can't stress that too much.

We are checking the records now, and I must say the task is astronomical. In this city alone, drunks, alcoholics, and heavy drinkers have wrought havoc with innocent children and the elderly', not to mention man",' other members of this community." Miller paused to check his notes, and continued. "That is where we are to date, gentlemen." He sat down, and lit another cigarette.

Captain Winters stood after Miller was seated. He began, "Starting today', designated department personnel will contact members of the police departments in the areas where the murders took place. You will gather data, compare notes. All police departments have pledged to cooperate in this investigation.

We need each and every one of you, whatever your expertise, to go back through the evidence gathered so far."

"How will we know what is pertinent?" someone asked.

"You won't. But if you're in doubt, check it out, and if necessary recheck it. It won't be easy," he said. "So far, nothing about this case has been easy."

The meeting ended with everyone pledging to help in any way he could.

Miller and his men spent the following weeks going through the evidence and the very slim clues.

They were able to piece together a gossamer pattern that had many holes and doubts. Miller had many questions that were unanswered, I put one stood out: what was the killer like? Obviously he was able to function and present a good facade to the public. Miller decided to talk to Dr. Yeager about the problem.

Miller had a folding bed in his office. Tonight he lay dressed in trousers and shirt. As he often did, he thought of his wife - her long illness, and his relief when she was released of her suffering by death. It had ended his interest in the outside world, and he had retreated into police work.

He realized the assassin was more than just a conventional murderer. He was clever, had done extensive research, and knew his victims and their movements. He groaned and turned to face the wall, burying his head deeper into his pillow. His thinking was becoming fuzzy, and be fell into a troubled sleep.

Miller said to Dr. Yeager, "You've read about the killings in the past few months?"

"Yes, who hasn't?"

"What kind of personality are we dealing with?"

"I can only give you a general description of this person, because I have not met him and had the opportunity to examine him."

"I know that, Doc. Just off the top of your head," Miller said as he lit a cigarette.

"In my learned opinion-and off the top of my head-I think we are dealing with a pathological grief reaction. We all know that grief is a normal phenomenon and an essentially healthy restitutive process, but some individuals are unable to experience it properly."

"You think our man is still experiencing grief of some sort and it involves alcoholics or heavy drinkers? A Miller asked.

"You're probably right. You see, persistent absence of emotion following the death of a loved one represents the effort to avoid the intense distress of grief. In such cases, grief will be expressed in clearly pathological or disguised ways."

"Which explains his killing a particular segment of the of the population."

"You're on the right track. His grief may be displaced, as in an obsession with the deceased. It can be transformed into a neurotic identification, as when the mourner avoids activity and the joys of living and lives as one dead. It can be delayed for 5'ears in some patients who undergo acute bereavement after the death of a loved one."

"That son-of-a-bitch. The first murder occurred around three years ago.

"What's that, Hugh?"

"Oh, nothing, Doe. just a passing thought."

"Hugh, unduly prolonged grief reactions tend to become ends in themselves in the survivor's effort to deny the loss. One form is idealization of the lost person so that unpleasant features of the relationship will remain repressed."

"Uh huh. Go on."

"In acute grief reaction-and I think that's what we have here-the grief occurs in response to the loss of a loved one l)y death. It's different from pathological depressive reactions in that the loss may be real or fancied, and ma",' be precipitated by various causes. Self-esteem is drastically lowered and repressed behavior occurs.

"This seems to suit the suspect I have in mind-the poor bastard."

"I'll give you three manifestations of grief: One. Intense preoccupation with the image of the deceased, accompanied by a feeling of unreality and an increased emotional distance from other people.

"Two. Disconcerting loss of warmth in relationships with other people, with either an aloof manner or irritability and anger.

"Three. Loss of normal patterns of conduct, with restlessness, inattentiveness, absentmindedness, and a painful lack of capacity to initiate and maintain organized patterns of activity. He may appear to be aloof."

"Thanks, Doc, this certainly accounts for the premeditated, cold-blooded murders we have encountered. I don't know about manifestation number three. So far his organization and execution have been right on the money. No clues, only suspicion on my part."

"Well, Hugh, you'll find a way. You always do. Is there anything further?"

"No, you've been a big help," Miller said as he walked away.

CHAPTER V

Jonathan, dressed in robe and slippers, was shaving when the doorbell rang. He started to answer the bell; as he went he wiped the lather from his face. He opened the door and said, "Yes?"

Lieutenant Miller and Detective Brown stood at the apartment door.

"I'm Lieutenant Miller, Homicide Central Division, and this is my colleague Detective Sidney Brown. \\'e would like to speak to you about the Stephens murder."

"How can I help?"

"May we come in?"

"Yes, of course. Come in, gentlemen." He stepped aside to allow them to enter.

After they were inside, he said. "\\'on't you l)e seated?" Both men sat on the couch. He continued, "Can I get you some coffee?"

"No, thanks."

Well, now, what can I do for you?

Miller asked, "We're you a guest at the Stephenses' dinner patty?"

"Yes, I was-a guest of a guest. I came along with an invited friend."

"As you probably already know, Air. Stephens was killed after midnight."

"Yes-I read about it in the paper.

"We are investigating the Stephens case and some other related deaths you might have read about."

"I've seen the newscasts and read the newspapers, but I have no idea how I can help you. My meeting with the Stephenses was my first. As for the others, I can only tell you what I've read." Sidney Brown said, "You might have seen something unusual, anything that seemed out of place."

"I am sorry, no." He paused and then said, "I've read that the murders in three or four states are all similar, and caused by one man.

Miller said, "Of course, it is always possible the deaths could be related, but that has to be proven." He crushed his cigarette in the nearest ashtray.

Jonathan relaxed mentally, and said, "The newscaster mentioned a distinctive odor, a sweetish smell. I did not detect an odor of that kind."

"I did not necessarily mean that," Sidney said. There might have been another unusual occurrence- remark you might have heard and did not pay too much attention to at the time."

Jonathan nodded and said, "I understand what you are saying, and I *am* sorry I cannot be of help to you.

"I'm sorry to raise a painful subject," Miller said. "We've checked the records up to three years back; we found that your family was involved in an 'Auto vs. Auto.' A drunken driver was responsible for the deaths of your wife and children."

The statement hit like a fist to the solar plexus, and Jonathan winced visibly. When he had regained his equilibrium, he said simply, "Yes, that is true, Lieutenant."

"We would appreciate it if you could, at your earliest convenience of course, drop into police headquarters for a talk," Miller said.

Jonathan thought, *So this is ": 'hat he's after*. Aloud he said, "What can I possibly tell you, Lieutenant?" He waited for Miller to respond.

"I'm sure you are aware of the astronomical undertaking of trying to find the so-called Extract Killer. We are hying to eliminate as many suspects as possible, and this is one of the means. The sheer number, at times, is mind boggling."

"I will be glad to help in anyway I can," Jonathan replied. "Will tomorrow be soon enough?"

Miller said, "That will be fine, thanks."

"You think it is someone from this group doing the killings?"

"It's one possibility."

"So, I guess that makes me a suspect'

"Yes, I guess it does."

"This town is full of kooks, Lieutenant."

"You got that right." A smile appeared on Miller's face as he prepared to leave. "I'll see you tomorrow, Mr. Loring. Here's my card."

Sidney said, "Mr.. Loring, I hope we have not taken too much of your time?"

"No-no-I am only sorry I could l)e of no assistance.

"You have my card," Miller said, as lie handed Jonathan his calling card. "Just call either one of us at that number if you happen to remember anything." He and Sidney walked to the door, with Jonathan following.

Jonathan said, "I will, Lieutenant." He moved around the two men and opened the door and smiled. "Good-bye, Lieutenant, Detective Brown."

He closed the door, and reflected momentarily on the meeting.

He remembered looking down on the body of Stephens. He also thought of the buoyancy be felt as he crossed the terrace and entered the garden.

He had expected the killing to create more excitement. Instead, the news account was disappointingly short. He anticipated more conversation at the marina that would allow him to luxuriate in omniscient glory; but that did not happen. Only days after Stephens's death, gossip veered away to a dozen other shallow subjects. There were no accounts of the autopsy in the tabloids.

He should have been happy, but he could not be sure the police were not onto something. Instead of being happy and toasting himself, he knew only a dull, leaden, let-down feeling. His depression became worse when he closed the door to his apartment.

He went directly into the bedroom and opened the closet door. The small leather case nestled in its hiding place on the top shelf. He walked over to the bed and unzipped it. Fitted into neat, recessed niches were a large syringe, two cardiac needles and two vials. He touched the contents before closing the case. He decided at that moment to find a better place of concealment.

Jonathan smiled sardonically because he had recognized the lieutenant and Detective Sidney Brown. The same team had investigated his family's deaths. He could not be sure they had remembered him, because his appearance was not the same.

He opened the bedside table and removed the news clippings of the accident that took his family.

He caressed the last reminiscence of his wife and children on earth, and for the ten-thousandth time he read them again, before putting them gently' away.

The uncertainty' of the police in their investigation of the deaths and their assumption that the killings were committed by a maniac never ceased to amaze him. He said softly, "I have never thought of myself as a maniac.

He remembered all the mysteries he had read while growing up. He thought of the men who failed where he had succeeded. He wondered how many were successful. There were times when his daring overwhelmed him. He had to remind himself that he had gotten away with murder, and at times he would say it quietly. "I have gotten away with murder."

CHAPTER VI

The most bizarre chain of murders to surface in a decade has left over seventy men of great wealth and power dead.
The first killing took place over thirty-six months ago. The deaths were first documented at that time.

Investigators suspect the killer has had a tragedy in his life, quite possibly involving an alcoholic. The victims are most vulnerable when they are drinking heavily. Alcoholism has a mortality rate of one hundred percent if not treated.

To recent years institutions for the treatment of alcoholism have mushroomed throughout the United States.

Communities large and small have seen manifestations of this disease; it has reached epidemic proportions. New cases are reported annually: the numbers have doubled in the last decade.

The most tragic victims of alcoholics are the children and the elderly.

This disease is becoming the most important and preventable cause of major injuries and death. The spread is fast, striking down over 26,000 per year. Statistically, we the public see just the tip of the iceberg. Most statisticians are afraid there are many more than the reported cases.

The problem must be dealt with and solved. Our court system is not the answer.

What is the solution? The court system must get the violators into meaningful programs. Doctors should take their heads out of the sands, so to speak, and give meaningful and effective treatment, instead of covering alcoholism with other diagnostic symptoms.

Insurance companies must get involved and recognize that alcoholism is an illness, and in essence help pay the bills.

Alcoholism is one of our nation's leading health problems.

So, fight alcoholism with understanding and effective treatment.

Lieutenant Miller tossed the newspaper on bis desk after reading the editorial and lit another cigarette from a smoldering butt. He rubbed his tired red eyes and settled back, deep in thought. There was something he had missed, something or someone to tie these deaths together. The clue was there; he just couldn't see it. He did not have the faintest idea what it could be.

There was an elusive fragment of thought that stayed tantalizingly out of reach, in the recesses of his mind.

He said out loud, "To hell with this!" and lapsed back into thought. After seeing so many killings it took great effort to be enthused anymore. *"What difference could one man make?* He didn't really mean that. There was always one more or a dozen more deaths. In disillusionment, he rose quickly from his chair, grabbed his coat, and left his office. He needed a change of scene badly.

Later, Miller met with Sidney.

"Sid, sometime back, almost three years ago, a young mother and her two children were killed.

The car she was driving was struck by a drunk driver. You and I investigated the accident."

Sidney said slowly, "Guess-yes, I do-Andrew or-" lie snapped his fingers trying to remember. "Adam something or other."

"Adam Lockhardt - walked away with only minor lacerations and scratches." Yeah, now I remember the guy. Tried to give us money. What about it?"

"The description is of a tall, slender, well-dressed man of about the right age. The deaths started a few months after the Loring deaths." lie paused and then continued to speak. "Where has he been-all this time?"

Sidney said, "Well-let's find out. Stampley may have something in his notes. 01' Stamp keeps careful notes." He searched through the accumulated notes that related to the case. "Ah, yes. Here's the report."

"How are you coming with the list of suspects?" Miller asked.

"We're progressing slowly but surely. Why don't I have Stampley come in, and you 'and he can wade through his notes. He keeps good notes, but only he can read them."

"Yeah, send him in," Miller said.

Stampley arrived moments later, wiping sweat from his brow, wheezing, his suit rumpled. He always gave the impression of being in a hurry. He sat across the desk from Miller.

Miller spoke first. "How are you coming with your investigation "I'm progressing. I'll make this as brief as I can."

"Take your time. I want a thorough report."

"Okay. So far this is not turning out to be an ordinary series of murders. It's spectacular, if one can call murder spectacular. Shooting and knifing someone is one thing; that's done all the time. But this guy and these killings are particularly vicious. All the same MO."

"Uh huh. Go on.

Stampley tried to cross his legs and finally settled for tucking one ankle behind the opposite knee.

He said, "This seems more like a vendetta against drunks and alcoholics. I've checked with the police departments in the other cities and the facts lead me to believe we are dealing with a crazed man-no, a madman. This guy has no conscience-and probably no remorse. He has brought enough attention to him self."

"But-" Miller started.

Stampley raised a pudgy hand, palm forward. "No, bear with me on this. This is textbook psychology. This killer is not our ordinary weirdo. I also have a feeling he wants to be caught. He'll probably become so disturbed he'll start writing letters soon."

"He's already done that," Miller said, and he handed the letters to Stampley. "See what you think of these."

Stampley read the letters through.

"These prove me night. Don't you agree.?"

"Up to a point." Miller paused. "Let's have your report."

"How about some coffee while I get my notes squared away?" He brought out his notes and started to leaf through them as Miller walked over to the coffee maker, filled two cups, and returned to his desk with them.

Stampley took a large, slurping drink and said, "I've checked through all the numbers as they happened. Numbers one and two took place in Aspen, Colorado, early in the ski season, thirty-six months ago. From there I checked with the Monterey Police. Numbers three and four occurred during the Concours d' El6gance, a rally of vintage cars. The next report came from Carmel, California. The Bach Festival, held each July in Sunset Center. This two-week festival brings some of the world's finest musicians to the Monterey Peninsula."

"Obviously some heavy drinking is done," Miller cut in.

"This fellow must have resources. He frequents sonic of the better places." Miller lit a cigarette. "Yes, that is true. There was another in the South Lake area of Tahoe, Emerald Bay, a very picturesque location. The body was found at Eagle's Point, where it juts out into the water. This corpse had a grand view of the Nevada shore."

"Funny. Go on," Miller said.

"San Francisco. Now, he really had a field (lay there. There were several, six to be exact, the first at Half Moon Bay, at the Art and Pumpkin Festival. One in Coit Tower, overlooking San Francisco Bay and the Bay Bridge." Stampley stopped to turn the page then continued. "The next on Lombard Street, as it snakes its way between I~lyde and Leavenworth. This corpse was stretched out in the hydrangeas.

Another in Ghiradelli Square, on a bench near the splashing fountain, a good view of the sailboats in the l)av. There was one near St. Francis Yacht Club: a doctor in his car, near Crissy Field. The last was found in the john at the Fainnont Hotel's Crown Room."

Miller around his cigarette out in the overflowing ashtray. "A regular travelogue of murder."

"Wait - that's not all" ,Stampley wiped more sweat from his face.

"Yegad! There's more"-"Miller asked.

"This guy started out killing affluent drinkers, but how it doesn't matter. Any publicized accident involving alcohol seems to be fair same. I'm looking into that angle now so far he's varied from his M.O. only twice. Two victims were killed by injection the substance into the base of the brain. Secondly, he stopped killing,, all super wealthy. Now it upper-middle and middle class."

"That's some report." Miller rubbed his tired eves and thought about having another cigarette but decided against it for the moment. He said, "Get back to me if you turn up anything else."

"Okay, fine." Stampley shoved his damp handkerchief into his coat pocket. He closed the door softly as he went out.

"Gonzalez Report." Miller turned the pages until he found the section he wanted. There it was, dated thirty-six months ago.

AUTO vs. AUTO
Three killed:
1. Stephanie Loring, thirty-two-year old mother.
2. David Loring, five-year old son.
3. Molly Loring, three-month-old daughter.

Jonathan waited across the street. He watched the doorway to the restaurant. Beside him on the front seat lay the *News Courier*, open to a four-column spread picturing Adam Lockhardt and his wife when they returned from Europe.

Lockhardt was a big spender who had an intense desire to be in the news. There was a summer home in Southern California, a fifteen-room bungalow in Maine. A recent editorial stated he was negotiating for a chateau in Europe. His business affairs took him and his family abroad several times a year. He wanted the biggest, the best of everything. His wife's shopping sprees were notorious: furs for every occasion, clothes from the leading fashion houses. Their children went to the best schools.

Adam had an eye for the beautiful ladies, and women were dazzled by him. His only imperfection: he was the world's biggest boozer. He lived and acted like an omnipotent king and did seem to have the "Midas Touch." His business flourished.

His estate above the Hollywood Hills nestled between gently rolling, rich green hills; it offered a breathtaking view of the mountains. The mansion and guest cottages were set like ornate jewels around the well manicured grounds. A butler and caretaker were on duty at all times; a staff of servants traveled with or in advance of the family.

Jonathan waited patiently. The *News Courier* society page contained the story of the Lockhardts' evening out with friends at the "Fleur de Lys."

He checked his watch again, and settled back comfort-ably to wait. His automobile was parked in a shadowed area that allowed an unlimited view of the restaurant.

Several couples emerged, stood for a moment talking,. and then parted company.

Adam Lockhardt and his wife climbed into the waiting limousine. One couple passed within a few feet of Jonathan's Alercedes. They were laughing and chatting discreetly about the masked ball being arranged by the Lockhardts.

The chauffeur drove the limousine expertly and, it seemed, with little effort along the quiet suburban streets. time Jonathan followed at a discreet distance. He thought the would come for his revenge.

The heavier car reached its destination. The gates opened as if by magic. The Lockhardts entered the grounds to the estate and the car was swallowed by the darkness.

The only evidence from Jonathan's vantage point was two red tail lights as the limousine disappeared behind a large shrub. He smiled and drove slowly away.

Sid, you are going to think I've lost my senses, but I know who is committing the murders."

"You're kidding-who?"

"I'm almost certain this Loring is our killer."

"You're joking."

"I never joked about mass murder." Sidney listened. "He fits the description. I can't prove it, of course. The proof will take some digging."

"Have you told the captain?"

"No-not yet. Just think about it. The circumstances fit-this type of killing didn't start until three years ago. The physical description fits."

"You can't convict someone on that alone. There are thousands that fit the description."

"I can't prove it now, but I will," Miller said with intensity.

"How do you propose to do that-prove it, I mean?"

"With your help. I want to conduct a search of his apartment."

"What! We can't get a search warrant on your gut feeling."

"I know that. You have a problem going without a search warrant?"

"You bet your boots! Leave me out of that. We'd be committing a crime, breaking and entering." Sidney protested, but not too convincingly.

Lieutenant Miller and Sidney entered the apartment surreptitiously, late at night. They had watched Jonathan leave with friends for the evening.

Two hours later the two policemen had done a thorough search. They had tossed books from the shelves, torn the bed apart, turned back the rugs, thrown clothes on the floor. Be-fore leaving, they removed the television set, video recorder, expensive camera equipment, and other small items to make it appear to be a burglary.

When they were back in the unmarked car, Sidney said, "That was a lot of work."

"Yeah-too bad nothing turned up."

"You didn't really expect to waltz right in there and find the stuff lying there, did you?"

"No-not really-but it was worth a try."

"*You* think we should have taken all that stuff?"

"You know, if we take some things, it's a burglmy. If you don't, it's a search. We couldn't make him suspicious. Besides, we'll wait a while and then find the stuff, call him in, and return it."

"So, where do we stand now?"

We never moved. We're still at square one, but you have to admit it was worth the tty.

"Yeah, if we'd found something, we would be winners, instead of sitting here with these foolish expressions on our faces," Sidney said.

"It's him-I feel it." Miller answered. There was a long pause and Miller asked, "What do you suppose he was doing all these months?"

"Well, hell, you could always ask him." Sidney replied, and continued, "Oh, sure I'll go along wit h you on a few of your assumptions. Granted, there were instances where a tall, slender, well-dressed man was seen, but that is not conclusive. There are thousands that fit the description. He could also be the killer because the deaths started after his family was killed, *hut* we have a long list of people whose lives were taken in the same manner. Your gut feeling is not enough. We need proof."

"You're right." Miller stopped as if considering something of importance. He said, "Do you realize I have not had a cigarette?"

"Yes, I knew the fog had cleared for some reason," Sidney said, and he changed the subject. "Why don't we talk this over with the captain?"

"Okay-but I think we should keep an eye on him." He lit a cigarette, his first in two hours. "All right by me-the fog is back."

The suite of offices occupied the third floor of the Mirror Building, which covered one square block in downtown Los Angeles.

The victim was a tall, angular man an inch or two above six feet tall. His dark hair had touches of gray at the temples. He lay on the thick carpet. His respiration's were labored and loud, as he gasped for air. The light was diffused; everything around him was hazy. His eyes would not focus. His body settled to the floor in death; the few muscle twitches finally stopped.

Jonathan watched the final throes of the agonizing death. He then serenely stepped over the corpse and left the office. Closing the door quietly behind him.

Letter # 3:

Judge Deerbome:
I am sorry I didn't warn you earlier about Arthur Gage, ALCOHOLIC. The court system has fallen short of its intended goal: to protect the innocent.

Judges of your kind lecture and give minor slaps on the wrist. Few drunks are charged, and even fewer are convicted. Many are allowed to plead guilty and are then released back into the streets to cripple and kill again.

I consider it my duty to clear the streets and highways of this garbage.

Outraged Deerborne held the telephone receiver tightly and said, "Lieutenant Miller?"

"Yes, this is Lieutenant Miller. May I help you.

"This is Judge Deerbome. I have received another letter. This time it was shoved under the door to my chambers. I will send it over to you.

"I'd appreciate that, Your Honor."

"How is the case progressing?" "We're making some progress.

"Keep me posted. I feel some responsibility about these deaths."

"You are following the law, Your Honor."

"But, still, if I hadn't allowed them to go free-"

"The publicity seems to be the key factor."

"Yes, I suppose. Well, keep me posted, Lieutenant." That ended the conversation.

Miller sat across from Captain Winters. He lit a cigarette and said, "I have a theory. I want to get your response."

"All right. I guess everybody had his own pet theory. So, whats yours?"

"Three years back, Sidney and I covered an accident, Auto vs. Auto, involving a young mother and her two children. They were all killed outright, pronounced dead at the scene. The husband, Jonathan Loring, was a distraught and angry man."

Winters interrupted. "I can see why. He had a right to be angry, especially under those circumstances."

"I know-but he was different. He disappeared shortly after the funeral."

"So?"

"Just hear me out. He had apparently cleaned up money wise, 'from this grave misfortune." Miller leaned forward to extinguish his cigarette.

"So, what's your point?"

"I'm getting there - I'm getting, there. He had a smart lawyer who was his friend. This friend was looking toward the future. He sued Adam Lockhardt, who paid willingly We checked back and found the sale of Lorings home, and a large lump sum, settled by Lockhardt."

"Conscience money," the captain interrupted.

Miller continued. "All this was invested by said attorney. Now we find that our Mr.Loring is a very wealthy man. We also know Loring is an engineer and knows all out substances. He graduated near the top of his class from Stanford University, where he majored in engineering with a minor in science."

"So far, you've given me a good history. I still say-so what?"

"Can't you see it? His hobbies include skiing; murders were committed at a well-known ski resort. He sails; San Francisco is noted for its sailing. He plays tennis with the wealthy and is aware of their weaknesses. He is a music buff; he was at the Bach Festival, where there were other murders. He's done some mountain climbing. He's athletic."

"Can you prove he's the killer?"

"No-but I'm working on it." He lit another cigarette, then saw the look on Winter's face. "Don't say it-I know I smoke too much."

"Tell me about it."

"Okay. Now, the description of a tall, slender, well-dressed man on more than six occasions fits him to a T. Sidney and I questioned him recently. He has changed in physical appearance. He's thinner, has grown a mustache and a neatly trimmed beard. He did not turn a hair when he saw us. He's deathly calm; it was as if he did not recognize us. He either *has* forgotten or he is a super cool character. The timing is right. There is one thing that puzzles me.

"What's that?"

"Why would he kill all the others? I would expect him to go after Lockhardt."

"Maybe that's what he wants to do."

"You agree he could be in Los Angeles to kill Lockhardt, and the other killings are just window dressing?"

"Who knows, he *could* be the killer and it *could* be a thousand other people. You gave me a theory-your theory but you can't prove any of it."

"No-not yet. We need to keep Lockhardt under surveillance for a while."

"I don't have the men to spare."

"We can do it, Sidney and I."

"I can't spare you either.'"

"We could do it in our spare time.

Winters said thoughtfully, "I don't know; you could be wrong. This could be just some nut who doesn't like drunks."

Miller took the last cigarette, crumpled the pack, and threw it into the waste basket. He said, "Wouldn't surprise me. I don't have a corner on being right. But what is so wrong about my theory? It all fits."

"Granted, it might fit, but you will have to admit, there are a lot of documented victims of dipsomaniacs that won't mourn their deaths." He paused and then said with feeling, "What ever happened to the funny drunks? Where, on Saturday night, Uncle Ned gets falling-down drunk and gives everybody a good laugh. *These* drunks go on a tear and kill innocent people. In this city, people see the drunkenness and rush on or look the other way!"

Miller remarked, "There are groups out there to help."

"Those places are only after money; they'll only take them in if they are well heeled."

"*You know* the system could remedy some of this slaughter on our streets. Judges could dispense better-thought-out sentences. Doctors could prescribe better treatment programs. I could go on and on, but I am sure you ret the idea."

Captain Winters said, "What was it Stampley said? A vendetta? This character was probably deranged in some way to begin with; otherwise he should have been able to handle his loss, if it was a loss. Who knows? He could bear another kind of grudge. He may have been abused as a child by a drunken father-or a rich drunken uncle. There are a whole flock of people in *this city* alone who could have done all the murders and walked away without a backward look. There are all sort of crazies loose now days."

"There's a difference," Miller stuttered. "Not all people have traveled the places he has. I still have this gut feeling that if we watch Lockhardt, we '*will* get our man.

"It might work, and then again it might not. Since you feel so adamant about it, give it your best shot. But for only a while. You will have to keep things in perspective."

CHAPTER VII

Sidney sat across from Mrs. Gardner, and Miller stood on the ten-ace outside the glass doors that led to Mrs. Gardner's living room. It overlooked a sparkling clear lake and across to the mountains beyond.

Miller said, "The view is magnificent," as he leaned on the balcony railing.

"I like it; it's very restful. But you aren't here for the view. How can I help you?"

Miller entered the living room and sat across from her. "Have you heard from your nephew-in law, Jonathan Loring, recently?"

"No, I haven't, but my daughter said she'd read about him in the news. He had attended a gala given by sonic industrialist."

"Has your daughter seen him in person?"

"No - I'm sure she hasn't. She would have told me if she had."

"Where can we contact your daughter?"

"Oh, you can't-not for some time. She left for Europe two days ago."

"Is there a hotel or some place we could reach her by phone?"

"I'm afraid I can't help you. Her itinerary takes her to some out-of-the -way places, but when I hear from her, which should be soon, I'll have her contact you, if that will help."

"Immeasurably. Here's my card. You can reach one of us day or night. Can you tell us something about Mrs.. Loring?"

"I was so sorry for Jonathan when his family was killed. He was so alone. We asked him to stay with us, but he refused. I knew that wasn't good for him in the state he was in."

"What do you mean, 'the state he was in?"

"He'd changed right before my very eyes. I could see he was an angry man. He needed to see a therapist, but he refused. I have never seen anyone endure the kind of mental anguish that he went through. He, Stephanie, and the children were a close family. When they were gone and the 'way they died-it left him filled with rage."

"Did you know anything about his background?"

"Some. His parents were killed when he was very young. He was raised by an uncle and his wife. The uncle's wife was not an affectionate woman. As a matter of fact, she was very cold." She paused and continued in a pensive mood. "Jonathan led a lonely childhood. Until he met Stephanie, he was a lonely young man. When the children were born, his life seemed so complete. He was the happiest, most considerate father and husband I have ever seen.

"Where did he meet his wife?"

"They met at Stanford University and soon developed a close relationship. They were married after graduation."

"How did he react after the funeral?"

"He could not accept it; he blamed himself. He seemed preoccupied with the idea of death. He withdrew and appeared very disturbed, wouldn't talk about the deaths. Lieu-tenant, you have to understand his family was his life."

"Did he comment at all on his feelings?"

"That was the most difficult time for us all. Jonathan was devastated. I always thought he should have talked to someone about it, but he held it in. He never shed a tear, he was too calm. He gave the impression at times of not being affected by his grief, but he was deeply hurt.

"I'm sure he has had a rough time," Miller commented..

"Yes." She paused and then continued. "You know, gentlemen, the death of Stephanie and the children was not the only tragedy in Jonathan's life. He lost his parents in a similar accident, as I said, when he was ten or twelve. He was brought up by his uncle, his father's brother, and his wife. I understand the uncle's wife was so selfish. Didn't pay any attention to the youngster.

"Jonathan withdrew into himself. All through high school, he was brilliant, but he had problems with relationships.

"In college, he met Stephanie, my sister's daughter, and she was what he needed. His life had meaning, and when the children arrived, they were the happiest family around. He had a good position-I mean, a job with a brilliant future."

"Did his parents leave him any money?"

"Yes, they left some. His uncle invested it."

"But it wasn't enough to buy a yacht-and travel as he's been doing the past two years."

"No. But, you know, after the accident, our attorney took over for him-the poor boy-and negotiated a settlement from the other driver. He also sold the house and made some wise investments. Jonathan would never have done that, but, you know, we have to go on living. The money did allow him to get away and pull himself together. We've lost touch since then."

"You've been very helpful. Mrs. Gardner, thank you. If you think of anything else that might help, please call us." He reminded her of his concern and departed.

The condition of Jonathan's apartment had had an unsettling effect on him. He had reported the loss to the local police, and they were investigating the incident.

He said to the police officer, "I came home; the front door was ajar."

"Was there anything missing?" the officer asked.

"Yes-this is a list of the missing items, with the serial numbers." He passed the list over. "Did they have an ID number?"

"Yes-that's the number, the second on the list."

"Thank you, Mr.. Loring. We'll be looking for your belongings."

Jonathan opened the outer door and said, "I realize that could be difficult."

"Sometimes it is."

"Good night, Officer," Jonathan said as he closed the door and turned to survey the mess. We'll, he thought, *this can 'wait until morning.*

CHAPTER VIII

Jonathan was being followed when he left his apartment. He led his shadow through the park and into the downtown area during the height of the shopping day. His shadow stayed a prudent distance behind, and when possible, he followed from across the street, always keeping his prey in sight.

Jonathan ate lunch at a sidewalk cafe, aimlessly wandered for forty-five minutes, and then suddenly stepped out of sight.

The detective lost sight of him when he turned onto Chester Street from Main. The detective spent over thirty minutes tracing and retracing the nearby streets and buildings from Chester to Main, but no Jonathan. A perturbed flatfoot gave up. Resigned, he plodded to the nearest telephone booth to call the lieutenant, who would have his buns on a platter. A very irritated young detective approached the public telephone in a nearby shopping mall. As he walked along glumly, he saw Jonathan Loring calmly sitting on a bench, enjoying the warm, sunny day.

Loring smiled and said, "Nice day isn't it?"

The young detective replied, "Yeah, great." As he made his way across the park to the exit, he thought, *You slippery bastard.*

Miller opened the car door and plopped down onto the scat on the passenger side, and said to Sidney, "Not a damn thing!"

"You think I might be on the wrong track?"

"Hell, no!" Miller said. "I know I'm right. I feel it'.

"But, Lieutenant-"

Miller spoke as if to himself. "I know he's it. Everything fits, it has to be him."

"What was in the car.

"Nothing, just the damn registration." He slammed his fist against the dash. "Clean as a whistle." You can't kill anybody with a registration.

"I don't know what I expected. He's too smart to hide it where he lives or in the car, but we'll find it."

"What about his boat?"

"We'll get to that later."

Miller said, "You want to do a little extra duty tonight? I'm gonna watch that bastard myself, and someone should keep an eye on this Lockhardt character."

Will you calm down, for God's sake.:" Sidney said.

"We've broken departmental policy twice.

"You're going to have to reassess this situation and try another angle. You know, we did screw it up this time.

"All right, I'm sorry. I know I'm pushing too hard. Okay, what we do now is put the surveillance on hold for now go back to the beginning and go from there. I'm one hundred percent convinced he committed the killings, you know."

"I know that."

Resolve tightened across Miller's face as he lit another cigarette and inhaled deeply.

Having been rudely pushed into bachelor hood. Jonathan had become a creature of habit, and he followed a certain behavior pattern. He had become obsessed about his personal care, his living quarters, and his car.

He arrived home late, at three o'clock in the morning. There was a feeling of uneasiness, but due to the late hour, he ignored the apprehension at the time.

It was 9:00 A.M. Showered and freshly shaved, he wore a white velour robe. He sipped his first cup of coffee. He had several hours of sound sleep, but the anxiety persisted. He sat on the edge of his bed, staring at the arrangement of pictures of his family. It dawned on him that the radio station in his car had been changed; he never changed stations. He said aloud, "Miller, the son-of-a-bitch!" He dressed hurriedly and stormed out of his apartment to check his car. He looked through the glove compartment, the trunk; there was a strong odor of cigarette smoke. He found additional evidence that his car had been searched: several small items had been moved.

A sardonic smile appeared on his face when he noticed his neatly arranged pencil pad and registration had been moved. If the intruder had been aware of his meticulous neatness, he should have seen that all the articles were placed in a certain order.

Jonathan sat at the small bar with his second cup of coffee, analyzing this new development and making plans. He reasoned that Miller had been behind the search, or had done it himself. Not a shadow of doubt lingered in his mind. Then he thought, *it's more than likely because Miller's was shrewd.*

Jonathan surmised Miller would probably have him under surveillance. He wondered why he would go to such lengths to keep an eye on him. Where did he go wrong? What could Miller know or have guessed?

He changed his clothes and left his apartment. He had driven several blocks before he noticed the same dull green car following him. The car was not conspicuous, and he would not have seen it if he had not been alerted by the search.

Jonathan stopped at a restaurant, ate a light breakfast, and lingered over his third cup of coffee.

There was one older man sitting in a far corner who from time to time would glance his way. He had nursed the same cup of coffee throughout breakfast. He was an overweight, disheveled man with a slight wheeze when he breathed.

Jonathan paid his check and led his tail around the shopping plaza, to his haberdasher, a shoe store, a bookstore, then back to his parked car. He drove to a nearby parking garage and was walking away when the green car came through the parking gate. The driver was reaching for his parking ticket, dispensed by the automatic gate. Jonathan readily identified him as his follower, both men pretended disinterest in each other.

Stampley's brown hair was plastered to his head by the sweat that seemed to pour from his pores.

Jonathan did not want to appear that he knew he was being followed and did not try to shake the man tailing him.

He ambled along at a leisurely pace until he knew the man had resumed following him. He reached his intended destination thirty minutes later, and then browsed at the news counter in a drugstore, watched bowlers in a bowling alley, and read the silent stock quotation in a window of a bank before heading back.

They stood on the deck of the yacht and watched the hearse drive away toward downtown. The doctor stood at Miller's elbow and said, "Have you had any sleep lately?"

"Not much," Miller replied. "I can't figure out what's happening here; it beats the hell out of me.

Every time I think I have a line on this mess, there's another murder."

"Want me to give you something to help you sleep?"

Miller, as if he hadn't heard said, "Right on the yacht club grounds. People going and coming.

And on the deck of his own boat, out in the open. People see and don't see. Who finally found him? And did they notice anything?"

"His wife said he often drank alone and has favorite place was on his boat. She's over there talking to Sidney. Right now, you know all I know. The Extract Murderer strikes again. Smell that sickly' sweet odor? Hugh, you look like hell. Are you sure you don't want me to give you something?"

"I don't remember when I've had a good night's sleep. I was lying there staring into space when this call came in."

"I can give you something."

"All right, that should help. This case has me on edge. I'm always uptight, especially on this case.

I lie half awake most nights. I guess that's why I'm edgy."

"That's no good," Doc Gordon said. "Just half asleep. Medically it's no good. Here, take one of these."

"Okay. Thanks, Doc. You know how it is. During the day my thoughts are racing through my mind, and I can't stop them. When I lie down at night and relax a little, the brain keeps working."

"I know what you mean, but that's in your realm. I'm too busy with these damn killings, for Christ's sake."

"Why drunks?"

"How would I know?"

"I thought I had just about figured this thing out when the phone rang, with this murder. There has to be something I've missed. Anyway, someone on the news said that many people feel drunks need killing because they hurt people. It was an old woman, for Christ's sake. She says it's one less off the streets."

"So? You've a mixture of opinions; that doesn't mean they'll go out and do what this creep is doing."

"I guess-You're right; I am really tired. I think I'll take your advice and call it quits for today."

"You got another cigarette?"

"Sure." The lieutenant lit it for him. "We have so many suspects. We have eliminated the friends and close associates. That bonus us to the families that had a relative hurt or killed by a drunk driver or whatever the traumatic situations was, whatever it took to 8end this madman off."

The lieutenant took a short turn around the deck, peered into the cabin, and jammed his hands deep into his jacket pockets. He asked, "Okay, now. What about these pills you gave me to make me sleep? Do they really work?"

"Try 'em and see."

"Thanks, Doe See you." Miller waved good-bye as he ambled down the gangplank.

Jonathan had had dinner early and had settled down to watch the seven o'clock news. He sat before the television sipping his favorite wine. He leaned forward, his forearms resting on his knees. The TV reporter looked directly into the camera as he stood by the yacht *Isabel*. He was reporting that the victim had been killed on an open deck, before a number of people passing by. "So far no one has come forward that might have seen the killer."

Jonathan smiled. The reporter continued. "The wife's screams had sounded the alarm. She had apparently tried to awaken her husband. When she had attempted to shake him, his lifeless body fell to the deck. Her screams alerted club security, who then called the police. Mr. Jarman, head of security, said the man was dead when we arrived."

He finished speaking; the camera angle changed. There was a closer view of the yacht and the deck as the body was being moved. There was a shot of Lieutenant Miller as he left the yacht, surrounded by reporters clamoring for bits of news. He avoided cameras and microphones as he pushed his way forward. He said, "Okay, fellows, give me a break. We don't know the cause of death yet. You'll know when I know." With that, he climbed into his car and drove away, leaving the re porters behind.

Jonathan drank the last of his wine and chuckled.

He picked up the phone and dialed and said to the person who answered, "May I speak with Scott?"

"Scott, Jonathan. About that costume ball we were discussing. Is the invitation still open?"

"Yes. You're going, after all?" Scott asked.

"I thought about it; it will be a change. Is the ball special, like a certain period in history?"

"No, I don't think so.

"Good, I'll meet you and Julie for cocktails and go on from there."

"Great, Julie will love it. See you then."

The following article about the Lockhardts appeared on the society page:

A Costume Ball

It is anticipated to be the most lavish, fanciest dress ball ever planned in Southern California. The incredibly wealthy Mr. and Mrs. Adam Lockhardt will host the glittering affair in the near future.

Hundreds of invitations are being sent to dignitaries and their ladies. Guests will dine on cuisine from throughout the world. Chefs from Italy, France, Spain, and other far-flung countries will be on hand. The costumes, to name a few: Hamlet, Henry VIII, and Sir Walter Raleigh. Indeed, all the well-known characters of history and fiction will be represented.

Inside the mansion the guests will dance in the great hall to a twenty-five piece orchestra, along with several bands, string quartets, and a number of contemporary entertainers and comedians.

As the music plays, the guests will wine and dine on the finest foods and champagnes in drawing rooms that will be lavishly decorated. The staggering display of wealth will cost hundreds of thousands of dollars.

A famous costume designer has reportedly' been deluged with orders for his services. He said, "I have orders, so far, for two hundred of the dresses, and am increasing my staff by one hundred and fifty seamstresses."

European papers effusively report that a thousand costumes for an anticipated evening in California have been ordered. This number has probably never been rivaled.

A sampling of passersby was taken by our woman-in-the-street and it is the opinion that mobs of people will be lining the street outside the Lockhardt Mansion to catch glimpses of the rich and famous as they make their entrance.

Miller and Sidney left the city at one o'clock for an interview with a recent widow. They took the freeway out of the city. Ten miles south of the city they entered the foothills. By the time they parked in front of the two-story, fifteen-room home, it was one-forty-five. The two detectives mounted the broad steps leading to the front door. Miller rang the doorbell. The door was opened moments later by the maid. He said, "I'm Lieutenant Miller, Homicide, Central Division, and this is Detective Sidney Brown. We're here to speak with Mrs. Von Kirkson."

The maid opened the door wide. The detectives entered the spacious hall. She said, "Wait here, please. I'll get Mrs. Von Kirkson." The detectives looked around in awe at the opulence.

Gloria Von Kirkson entered the hall and said, "Please, won't you please come in and be seated?" They followed her into the book-lined library. The French doors were opened to a large patio, a formal garden, and, fmther out, an Olympic-sized pool. They sat facing Mrs. Von Kirkson on matching modernistic couches.

She said, "May I offer you a drink? I'm sorry, I don't know your names.

"I'm Lieutenant Miller and this is Detective Brown. We aren't allowed to drink while on duty, but you go ahead."

She walked to the bar, prepared her drink, and settled on the couch to sip the icy liquid. She asked, "How can I help you?"

Before answering, Miller studied her a few moments. Her appearance was pure establishment. She was in her mid-forties. She had carefully coifed auburn hair and dressed in muted shades of green. She probably tipped the scale at on hundred and five pounds soaking wet.

Miller, spoke. "Mrs. Von Kirkson, had your husband been threatened in recent months? Any crank calls?"

"No, not that I know of."

"Any enemies that seemed - particularly disgruntled? Past or present?"

"My husband rarely discussed his business or problems with his associates at home. I knew in general what the business was about, but he rarely ever talked about the details at home. His office records would indicate more about his work than I can."

"Do you know if your husband had any enemies in his company?"

"A hard-driving man like my husband couldn't help but make enemies, although I don't know of anyone angry enough to kill him."

"I take it he was rough at the office. How was he at home?"

"I don't understand, Lieutenant. What do you mean?" she asked coolly.

"Sometimes a person's home life will indicate or give clues to what goes on in the office."

A curtain seemed to close around the widow; there was a definite chill behind her green eves. She took a sip of her drink before answering. "My husband worked hard. We started with next to nothing. He has provided well for us."

"Were there any unusual occurrences recently?" Sidney asked.

"There was one thing. About six weeks ago we returned unexpectedly from dinner. As we drove into the driveway, I saw a light in the library go out. My husband stopped the car and ran into the front door. The burglar ran out the doors near the patio. I saw him running across the lawn. I yelled and my husband gave chase. It was hopeless; the burglar got away in a car. When my husband returned, I asked him if lie was going to call the police. He said he would after he determined what was missing. Later I asked him if he had called the police. He said no. He said since nothing was taken, the police couldn't do any good."

"Had there been other burglaries reported in the neighborhood?"

"Not that I know of, Lieutenant," she said sadly.

Changing his approach, he asked, "What kind of merger was Mrs. Von Kirkson working on?" She surveyed him several moments before answering. "That information is no longer relevant, Lieutenant. My husband's death ended that." She rose from the couch, the ultimate hint.

Miller said, "We appreciate you seeing us, Mrs. Von Kirkson, and I'm sorry to have taken so much of your time."

She didn't answer; she just walked ahead of them to the door.

During the drive hack to the city, Miller and Sidney tossed a few ideas around. Miller asked, "Well, what do you think?"

"I don't think she's the killer of her husband; their marriage was necessary to her."

"Yeah - Von Kirkson was more important to her alive. He catapulted a ten-thousand-dollar business into a twenty-five-million-dollar-a-year business.”

“She impressed me as being coolly determined, and she knows what she wants. Her ambition probably matched her husband’s.”

“My recent Inquiries indicate Von Kirkson seemed to have had a contended home life.”

“It was odd that he didn’t report the burglary to the police.”

“Omnipotent type.”

“The police don’t have a good batting average when it comes to catching burglars.”

“So, where are we?” A4iller asked. “Von Kirkson - ambitious, competent, content at home, played rough at work knew where he was going.”

“Mrs. Von Kirkson-a high achiever, contented with her marriage. Set for life.”

They both lapsed into silent contemplation as Miller maneuvered the car skillfully through heavy traffic.

Jonathan, awakened by his own loud moans from the nightmare he had lived with since the first killing, was drenched in sweat. He lay back to the gentle swaying of the boat. It seemed like a hundred years since his wife had been buried. Her image invaded his thoughts; his body ached for her. Words had always come easily between them. She could always calm his moments of stress by just being there. He could see her now, as she would come to him, touch, and kiss him. He’d take her in his arms; the urgency they would feel would consume them. The gentle rolling of the water on the beach would accompany their lovemaking. There was no doubt he loved his wife-and would until his dying day. Stephanie, so young, cut off from life. In his grief he said aloud, “Oh, Stephanie, I should have been there when you needed me most.” His voice was anguished.

Jonathan had accomplished the task of having his yacht moored in the slip alongside the James. It had taken some planning and money. Early Sunday morning he sat aboard the S.S.D.M. and waited for the owner to appear. He watched her for some time after she came out of the cabin. Her auburn hair glistened in the sunlight, and her slim figure made her appear tall.

He uncoiled his lean and muscular frame from the reclining position and moved with a catlike grace to the rail. He said, “Good morning.”

The young woman turned, startled, and said, “Oh-hello. I didn’t see you there.”

“I didn’t want to frighten you.

“You didn’t, really. I was not expecting to see anyone this early.” Her eyes were a warm brown, set in an open, friendly face.

"I'm an early' riser." He really was not, but what the hell. He continued. "How about this weather we're having?"

She said, smiling, in a sociable mood, "Isn't it great'.

"I am Jonathan Loring."

"Eleanor James. I'm pleased to meet you, Mr. Loring."

"Now that we're neighbors, can't we dispense with the 'Mr.'? Just call me Jonathan."

"To my friends and neighbors, I'm Eleanor."

He did not want to push things too soon. He said, "Well, neighbor, I must be off. Will yon be here long?"

"Yes - a few weeks."

"Then we must plan something together when you're free."

"Yes-let's," she answered, as he walked toward the park.

After dinner he took a leisurely walk along the marina to the clubhouse- and there she was, surrounded by her friends.

He said, "Hello, neighbor."

"Hi - Jonathan."

He smiled and walked on by, to return to the S.S.D.M.

He spent a wakeful night and had decided to see her again, but it would hardly be termed a romantic encounter. She was his sure entry into the social circle he needed at this time.

The next evening he knocked on her cabin door. No answer.

He continued to watch her yacht for the next five days. He had begun to panic. He wondered, *Did I misjudge her? Where is she!*

They met quite by accident a week later. He forced a smile as he fell into step beside her. He said, "Hello. I tried to reach you, to have dinner sometime."

She returned his smile and answered, "I've been away the last few days skiing."

"Oh, you ski? So do I. How was the skiing?"

"Conditions were very good."

"Are you free Friday night?"

"I'm not sure, but I will check my calendar and let you know."

"Why not look now?"

"I will have to let you know later. I have an appointment now."

"Okay - I'll be around," he said to her as she hurried away. He was pleased, his spirits lifted. She was back. Now he could make his plans.

Two evenings later he knocked firmly on her cabin door. She was dressed in a flowing, green dressing gown when she opened the door. She seemed surprised to see him. She thought, *You are the persistent one*. Aloud he said, "Won't you come in?" He walked through the door. She continued, "'Please sit. Can I get you a drink?"

"Yes. Scotch over ice."

She prepared it and brought the drink to him.

"Thanks." He took a sip. "No',; about Friday night."

He was direct, and he flattered her by his persistence. She sat across from him. There was no need for pretense; she was intrigued by the man. He had that effect on her.

"I was about to have dinner. Would you like some?"

"No, thanks. I have to run."

Her face brightened as she smiled and said, "Friday would be fine." He downed his drink. "Dinner at eight?" he asked as he stood to go.

"Yes." She was taken aback because of the abrupt departure. Eleanor followed him to the door. He said, "Good night."

"Good night, Jonathan."

"See you Friday."

"Yes-Friday."

After dinner, they were seated in the lounge aboard Jonathan's yacht. "What were you like as a little girl? Tell me about yourself." He smiled at her across the table.

She thought for a moment and then said, "There isn't much to tell. I grew up in Berkeley. From there, I went to Switzerland and England. When my parents died, I moved to Southern California. Not very exciting."

"You have relatives here?"

"Yes, an aunt in Palm Springs, cousins in San Clemente. What about you?"

"There isn't much to tell, my life has been spent in a way similar to yours, with only a few minor differences."

"Is there-that significant other in your life?"

"The right person, I think I have just met," he answered unashamedly. Eleanor was taken completely by surprise, and it showed on her face. Her mouth opened with the impact of his statement.

He continued, "When I first met you, I knew then."

"But-" she stammered.

He interrupted, "That's not so strange now, is it?" He moved beside her and continued. "You're the first person I have felt his way about for a long time. You are the one for me.

When he kissed her, she was completely overcome.

Eleanor was astonished and pleased by the quickness of the intimacy between them.

He stood, and in one swoop he lifted her into his arms and carried her into his customized stateroom, where he placed her on the bed and gently undressed her and hurried out of his clothes. Their passion rose with shocking intensity, as his ardent kisses fanned the flames of desire. He kissed her face and neck and then lovingly her breasts. He entered her. She uttered a muffled cry of pleasure as all her desire rushed through her. He had made her aware of her womanhood as no one else had in the past. She wanted him to hold her and love her.

When it was over she lay back in a state of languor to savor this moment. She thought, *What is happening to me?*

Eleanor had prepared brunch while Jonathan slept. She awakened him with a gentle kiss. He opened his eyes with some effort and smiled and reached for her. He held her in a long bear hug before getting out of bed.

The conversation during the meal involved an invitation to a dinner party given by the fabulously; wealthy Marcus de Fiat, who tossed glittering parties for hundreds of guests and whose friends included a host of Hollywood stars-and the Adam Lockhardts.

De Fiat's home was filled with priceless paintings and 'other art treasures. He was a member of America's legendaiy industrialist family and one of the world's richest men.

Before returning to his bungalow, Jonathan said, "Shall we make a day of it tomorrow?"

"Absolutely."

"Pick you up at nine o'clock."

"I'll be ready."

"I'll miss you, too." He held her close, her head nestled on his shoulder. "I'll miss you, too," she answered softly.

He kissed her lightly on the lips before releasing her.

In his bungalow, he checked his hiding place to see if everything was secure, and smiled his satisfaction.

Jonathan chuckled when he read the latest editorial:

EXTRACT KILLER STALKS FOUR STATES
FOR HEAVY DRINKERS

Los Angeles. Police are stepping up their hunt for a man labeled the "Extract Killer," who may have killed more than seventy-five heavy drinkers in a four-state area.

After two years detectives are frustrated because of the widespread murders. Lieutenant Miller believes the killings could have been started by one person and escalated to copycat killings.

"I also think," Lieutenant Miller said as he searched through piles of reports on hundreds of suspects, 'he's in this pile here." There is an indication that the killer may have shown up in the investigation.

Since the killings began, drnnkenness in the four-state area has declined precipitously.

Twenty-two bodies have been found in Southern California, and six more are listed as missing. The first eight bodies were found two months ago in suburban Los Angeles and the surrounding cities; others were from some of the area's most opulent homes.

All victims had histories of heavy drinking and had been arrested and tried at least once for either killing or crippling their victims.

The alcoholic victims had been injected with lethal doses of a three-part extract that created irreversible damage to the cellular structure throughout the body.

"It seems a foregone conclusion that the man will continue to kill until he gets caught. There are still six victims we can't account for," Lieutenant Miller said in an interview last week.

Officers are reviewing files on more than five hundred suspects and comparing them to past "serial killers"-people who kill singly in a series-such as the Hillside Strangler, in Los Angeles, or Son of Sam, in New York.

Lieutenant Miller has read books on mass murderers.. He also is working closely with an imminent criminologist, an expert on serial killings. Mr. Keith is a full-time Task Force consultant, and has said serial killers have such intense interest in the police and their investigation that they sometimes frequent places where the investigators gather and actually report bits of information to police.

They, the serial killers, all seem to have one thing in common: they move from place to place.

CHAPTER IX

Jonathan pushed the elevator's up button, and at that moment he saw a tail at the front of the building. Trying to appear nonchalant, he entered the elevator and ascended to the tenth floor.

Scott greeted him effusively. They Shook hands and slapped each other on the back. Jonathan asked Scott, "How is Julie?"

Scott smiled. "You know Julie, never a dull moment. God, you look great! What have you been doing?"

"Nothing. I've traveled a bit. I'm okay now."

"Glad to hear it."

"You said you had something for me to sign.."

"Oh, yes. I have the papers right here."

"What is it?"

"The transfer of funds you requested. i~our passport has been updated. And there are a few other transactions you should know about." He laughed and then continued. "I also haven't seen you for months. How have you been? Tell me about your yacht."

"I'm doing splendidly. I've seen halfway around the world, done and seen many things. You and Julie still have to spend some time with me on the *S.S.D.~II*. It's moored at the marina." He signed the papers as he talked.

"Let's set a date."

"Any time," Jonathan said as he stood to go.

"Is there anything further I can do?"

"No, I have everything under control now," Jonathan said, smiling lazily. He looked at his friend of many years and suddenly, instead of shaking his hand, he hugged him for a long moment and said, "You've helped me immeasurably already. Your friendship has always been there."

"Why don't we get together for dinner soon?" Scott asked.

"Just give me a call," Jonathan said, as be opened the door to leave.

The attorney followed him to the outer door and watched his broad back as he entered the elevator door. When his friend turned to face forward they both waved good-bye.

His tail still loitered conspicuously around the street-level lobby. He was so out of place, he received many long stares from passersby. He didn't deceive anyone by trying to appear nonchalant.

Jonathan exited the building with the intention of going home. On the way he zigzagged half a dozen times. He checked periodically to see if the detective was still there. The green car stayed doggedly a block behind. He deliberately parked a distance from his apartment and increased his pace 'to nearly a jog.

Stampley gasped for air as he kept his quarry in sight with difficulty. His handkerchief was saturated, as he had been repeatedly wiping the sweat that poured down bis face and neck. He exited a pedestrian pathway and noticed that Jonathan bad increased his pace and was nearly a block away. Disheveled and struggling for breath, he walked as rapidly as he could. He endured the fast pace for several minutes before he realized he had been led in a circuitous route and was back at Loring's apartment.

Jonathan saw the look of dismay on the detective's face and grinned evilly as the doorman opened the apartment building's outer door.

A TV' telecast flashed the following headline: "Drnnk Driver Released on His Own Recognizance."

Jonathan leaped to his feet in a blinding rage, and threw a pillow at the television. He spun on his heels, wrenched open the bedroom door, dressed angrily for jogging, and stormed out into the night.

He ran down the avenue to the beach. The raw emotion that had persisted all these months had intensified. He was not aware of time or place. He veered toward Terrace Walk and sat on the nearest bench, where he gazed, without really focusing, at the ocean. The night was clear, the sky star studded. The view was breathtaking, but for Jonathan, lifeless. He felt a sense of futility and crushing loneliness.

Like a crazed man, he sprinted home, thundered up stairs two steps at a time to his apartment, and hurled himself into the bedroom to pack. He was a man near the breaking point.

He rushed through his packing and then sat down for a moment to call Scott. He dialed, waited, and said, "Hello, Scott. Jonathan. I am going away.

"Where? What if I need you? Where can I reach you?" The attorney's voice was anxious.

"Ill be in touch."

"When? A week? A month? Is there any way I can help you now?"

"No-I can't tell you where I'll be. I do not know my-self-now."

"Jonathan-"

"I can't talk now; I'll call you soon. I have to get away.

"But, but-"

Jonathan dropped the telephone receiver and whirled back to the door where his luggage stood. He grabbed the bags, clattered down the stairs, strode through the hall, and burst through the outer door, grateful to be outside. In the car, he gunned the engine before driving out into the street.

The farther he drove from the cursed city, the more angry he became. The reckless drive had not calmed his emotions, but had served to enhance them. The anger he had felt earlier returned with an overwhelming rush.

He knew deep down that if his plan were to survive, he must calm down. No more irrational outbursts. His plans must not be jeopardized. He gripped the steering wheel so tightly that his knuckles blanched white. He said aloud, "He must pay. I'll see to it.

"Did Jonathan Loring ever tell yon how his family died?" Miller asked Eleanor James.

"Yes. He said his wife and two children were killed in an automobile accident caused by a drunk driver. Why?"

"We're investigating a series of deaths dating back over three years. We are also checking the living relatives and where they've been all that time."

"What does that have to do with Jonathan?"

"We don't know yet. We have to follow all possible leads, and Mr. Loring's misfortune happened in our time frame."

Eleanor said with disgust, "Hasn't he suffered enough? Do you have to open old wounds?"

"We're doing our job, ma'am. You've been seeing him frequently. Do you know where he spends his time when he's not with you?"

"A part of it. We're both free to do the things we want. There are no strings attached to either of us."

Sidney Brown asked, "Does he have other living quarters, other than his apartment?"

"He spends time on his yacht."

"Where is that moored?"

"The marina. The *S.S.D.M* I can't answer any more questions about his personal life. You will have to ask him."

Miller said, "You've been a great help, and we thank you very much, Ms. James." The two officers stood up. Sidney closed his note pad. They left without further questions.

The officers had been gone only moments when Eleanor dialed a number. She waited several moments before Jonathan answered. She said, "Jonathan?"

"Yes, speaking."

"This is Eleanor." She paused and then said, "Two policemen were here and asked me questions about yon, your past-especially about the accident involving your family."

"I guess that could be expected, because of all the killings in the news. They must be checking, as far back as three years ago. I wouldn't worry about it." He changed the subject. "Why don't you come over. I have something special for you."

Eleanor awakened from a deep sleep to the smell of brewing coffee. She smiled as consciousness took hold and she remembered where she was. The warm feeling took her back to last night.

She heard the clanking of dishes from the galley. She slipped quickly from under the covers and shrugged into an oversized robe.

She stood in the galley' door, observing Jonathan as he lazily prepared breakfast. When he notice her, he smiled and said, "Good morning. Coffee?"

"Sounds great."

"I'm going to the bakery, a couple of blocks away. What kind of pastry would you like?"

"A cinnamon roll will be fine."

Before she could say anything further, he passed by her, gave her a frindly pat on the derriere, and was on his way out the door.

She was taking a hot shower when Jonathan returned. He yelled to her that he was back, and that he would heat the pastry if she wanted him to. She did, and he popped them into the microwave.

When she joined him, she still wore the role. Her hair was wet, her face scrubbed clean.

She sat down across from him and said, "Cream, please."

He said, "You know, you remind me at times of the two most special people in my life."

"Oh - really? Who?"

"My mother. As a woman who dabbled in the arts, the theater, she was a bubbly', happy woman. She married my father young.

"I'll take that as a compliment. Who is the other?"

"My wife - Stephanie. You are like her in many ways. She was special because I could always tell her my problems."

"I'm flattered."

"There the comparison ends, because yon are a unique, multifaceted, personable young woman-all woman.

"What about your father? What was he like?"

"He was an insurance executive in San Francisco. He made a name for himself early in the insurance business. My parents were always understanding and sensitive to my needs as well as one another. I think I was eleven when they were killed on the Nimitz Freeway. A freak accident."

"I'm so sorry."

"Then I went to live with my father's brother, Uncle Gilbett, and his wife, Carolyn." He paused as if in thought and then continued. "There were times when I felt my parents' loss very deeply."

"What was your aunt Carolyn like?"

"Self-centered. Didn't want to be bothered with a young, energetic boy. And I could never have friends over. Soon after school started, I was an outsider in the neighborhood. I spent a lot of time alone."

"How terrible for you."

"Oh - not so bad. I made excellent grades, top of my class. School days were agony. Aunt Carolyn had a weird sense of humor when it came to dressing a young boy. I was new to the school. I was among a group of boys, most of whom made fun of the clothes I wore. Don't get me wrong. I was always well groomed, but I didn't dress like the in crowd."

Eleanor looked at him with great concern.

He continued. "Don't look so sad. I graduated with honors in mathematics and science. In the yearbook I was named the one most likely to succeed."

"Where are your aunt and uncle go?"

"Carmel."

"Do you ever see them?"

"I see Uncle Gil, but not Aunt Carolyn."

"Where did you attend college?"

He climbed out of bed to sit beside the bedroom window. Eleanor turned to one side to face him as he talked.

"I went to Stanford, the first taste of freedom in my life. You'll never know the feeling. That's when I found out what a bummer high school really was."

"Did you have many dates?"

"A few. Some of the young ladies were pseudo intellectuals, very transparent."

"And?" She didn't want to interrupt.

"Until I met Stephanie that afternoon in my second year. There was a chill in the air. Autumn leaves were falling. My body was alive that day. The air clean and crisp, the leaves rustled under my feet, and twenty feet away I saw Stephanie for the first time and I knew at that moment that this laugh-log, attractive-though not beautiful-woman would be a part of my future."

"That sounds so romantic.

He continued as if he had not heard her. "We didn't need anyone else because we had each other. We walked together, cut classes together, slept together. Our days at the university were very special. We were married shortly after graduation and the ten years we spent together were the happiest-" He paused and then said sadly, "All that was taken away three years ago. When a drunken driver slammed into her car." When he felt the renewed anger he stopped and changed the subject. "That's enough of that," he said. "Oh, by the way, are we still scheduled for the Lockhardts' costume ball?"

"Of course. You haven't changed your mind:" "No - I haven't."

She looked at her watch and said, "It's getting late. I must go. Will I see you before the party?" as she dressed to leave.

"Yes, I'll call you. Shall I drop you somewhere?"

"No, I have my car."

He walked her to her car, kissed her good-bye, and watched as she drove away.

Back in his living room, he held the newspaper with Lockhardt's photograph. As he stared at that smiling face, his hatred burned within him.

"Mr. Lockhardt, I am Lieutenant Miller and this is Detective Sidney Brown, Homicide, Central Division.

"Yes - what can I do for you?"

"I'll come directly to the point: three years ago you were involved in an Auto vs. Auto that resulted in the death of a mother and her two children."

"Yes. But that's all over, and I paid for that-and I mean dearly."

"Well, sir, we are investigating the series of recent so-called 'Extract Murders.' You probably have read about them."

"How could I miss it? They're all over the news. What does that have to do with me?"

"We have reason to believe that your life may be in danger."

"What reason! I have not been involved publicly with intoxication in three years."

"In going through the records for the last three years, Miller said, "we uncovered many records and we are now in the process of warning people who were involved in accidents involving deaths by drunk drivers."

"You mean this fellow-what's his name?"

"Jonathan -

"Yes, Loring. You mean he may be the killer? But why did he wait so long, and why all the other killings?"

"We're only saying it's a possibility,"

"I think you're grabbing at straws, to cover your incompetence.

"You understand, we have to follow all leads. -The warning was to put you on guard."

"Why don't you leave the poor slob alone. Hasn't he suffered enough?"

"We're doing our job as best we can.

Lockhardt said, "Well, you could put more energy into catching the killer and stop using my valuable time."

"Thank you for your time," the lieutenant answered caustically. Miller and Brown stood to leave. As an after thought, Miller said, "Here's my card. If you need help or can give us more information, we can be reached at this number " They walked out, closing the heavy door softly.

Lockhardt ambled over to the bar and fixed a particularly strong drink. As he walked back to his desk, he read the calling card with a grimace and tossed it into the wastebasket, saying, "That takes care of that." He sat in his comfortable chair and swiveled to view the panorama of the city.

Hugh Miller said to Sidney, "I can see *why* Loring could hate Lockhardt."

"You've got a point there; he's the original Mr. Nasty. But Loring isn't alone; there are hundreds out there." He made a sweeping motion with one hand as he indicated the city all around them. "Any one or more of them could be doing the killings."

"I think he's capable of this kind of hatred. It borders on the pathological."

"And you can't prove any of it."

"That's because, damn it, he controls it."

"It's your theory, and you're stuck with it. You're help-less, and he knows it, and I think, if he is the killer, he'd want you to know he knows you can't prove it."

"He's out there laughing at us. Did he ever come in to headquarters? Miller asked.

"Yes, he was in.

"The guy has to be stopped; he must be caught," Miller said vehemently.

"Well, at least we agree on that," Sidney said wearily. "What are you going to do now?"

"I'm not sure, anymore. Keep looking, I suppose," Miller answered.

"Whoever the killer is, he's a crazy - someone who can't cope with his loss."

"Yeah - you got that right."

"You really think this character Loring is the killer. Why? What is his motive?" Captain Winters asked.

"His family was killed; he's bitter about their deaths. He's insane, unable to cope with his loss." Miller lit a cigarette from another butt.

"Why wait so long and why kill all the others? Why not go directly to the one who killed his family?"

"He has gone over the edge with every accident involving drunkenness. They trigger the memory, and he's killing the person over and over that murdered his family."

"You're back on that same cockeyed theory: Loring's doing the killing. When are you going to let go?"

"I'll make a believer of you," Miller said as he crushed his cigarette out in the recently emptied ashtray. He said, "And - I smoke too much."

"I will say this for you: when you get an head you hold on like a bulldog."

"All right," Miller said. "It's crazy. For the time being, I have only a gut feeling, but I'll prove it eventually."

"Whatever you do, be thorough and be damn sure before you move on this. We need a helluva lot more than gut feelings."

"Time is my enemy, and the knowledge that he's always one step ahead."

"It takes old-fashioned legwork. You have the insight and all the latest police investigative equipment, but I want some-thing solid to go on.

"That's the name of the game."

"An example of good detective work is uncovering clues, testing theories, blind alleys, asking questions and more questions. You know all this; that's why I'm with you all the way.

"Thanks, Captain. My one concern right now is that the killer is probably in the midst of the so- called 'beautiful people' and selecting his next victim. He's being been and not seen."

"I'm always here if you need me," Winters said. "Thanks, Captain, I need your support."

Miller lit another cigarette before leaving the room.

The neighborhood was aglow as the sun sank over Southern California. The ranch house windows reflected the fading sunlight, and in the distance the sprawling home was silhouetted against the sky. A cool breeze brushed the surrounding trees. A tranquil setting on the edge of metropolitan Los Angeles. Every room in the Clayborn Mansion was a study in streamlined elegance, with the beauty of classic Italian architecture.

Benson Clayborn's assemblage of magnificent works of art was recognized as one of the finest collections in the world.

His body lay before a Florentine painting. Portraying the gods and goddesses of classical mythology Benson's sightless eyes were glazed in death as he breathed his last breaths, never to look upon the painting again. A slightly sweet odor lingered in the room.

The butler entered with the housekeeper. He immediately saw his employer struggling for breath. He moved to the stricken man on the floor and felt his pulse. He exclaimed, "My God! He's dying!" He turned to the housekeeper. I'll get the doctor and the police," he said as he lifted the telephone. "You call Mrs.. Clayborn."

The housekeeper stood there gaping at the dying man. Nelson shouted, "Now! Get a move on!" The housekeeper did not move. She said, as if in a trance, "He's dead."

Nelson shook her by the shoulders and said, "Will yon snap out of it and call Mrs. Clayborn!"

That was all it took to mobilize her into action. Her eyes cleared as she whirled and ran out the door., Nelson dialed the telephone. He said into the mouthpiece, "May I speak to Dr. Byers? Please hurry." He listened and then said, "Emergency. Mr. Clayborn is seriously ill. We need the doctor right away!" He waited again, impatiently. Moments later, he said, "Dr. Byers?"

"\'es, this is Dr. Byers. What's wrong Nelson? My nurse said something about Air. Clayborn being seriously ill?"

"We need you now, Doctor. I think he's dying."

"I'll be there right away!"

Mrs. Clayborn entered the room as Nelson broke the connection. She ran to her husband and shouted, "Clay! It's Edith." She took his clammy, limp hand in hers and said repeatedly, "Clay, it's Edith, honey. It's Edith. Everything will be fine, you'll see, Clay."

Dr. Byers found her kneeling there when he arrived. She was, moaning and crying, "Clay, please don't go, don't leave me.

The doctor lifted her bodily and helped her to a nearby couch. He instructed the housekeeper to stay with her.

Edith Clayborn clung tightly to the housekeeper's hand and moaned as she rocked back and forth, "Oh, my God. He's leaving me alone-Oh, God-"

Dr. Byers told Detective Vanness Goodman, 'He \vas dead when I arrived." Goodman stood beside the desk. lie said "I-low long had he been dead?"

"I'd say, within the last hour."

"Do you have an idea what caused it?"

"I am not sure, but there is an odd odor. I'm sure I can be more precise after an autopsy.

'Okay." Goodman turned and spoke to the photographers and technicians. "Do you have all you need here?" he asked.

They all answered in the affirmative.

Goodman picked up the telephone and dialed. He said, "Hugh Miller, please." I've waited a few moments and said, "Hugh? Van Goodman here." He listened and said, "I'm fine." Then he listened again and said, "It's not \"hat you can for me, but what I can do for you. I think we have one of your killer's victims here." He paused, and continued. "Yes-Benson Clayburn, according to the memorandum, I received from your office. There is an odor here, smells sweetish." lie listened for several moments and then said, "Okay I'll send you the report as soon as I get it." Goodman was silent. He smiled, and then continued to speak. "Yeah-when this is over, we'll get roaring drunk, like old times." He listened again, and then said, "Okay, later." Lie replaced the receiver softly.

Miller walked to the door of his office and yelled to Raymond, "Check out Loring. I want to know his every move the last twenty-four hours."

"Okay, Lieutenant. I'll get right on it," Raymond replied.

"Get back to me as soon as yon can.

Raymond shrugged into the jacket to his suit.

CHAPTER X

Jonathan was running far ahead of his pursuer, a hazy outline in the distance. He had reached the halfway marker and thought he had a commanding lead. Sweat poured from his pores and ran in rivulets down his face and chest. He took a quick look back over his shoulder and saw that the shadow in the haze was gaining on him, taking form. Anxiety flooded him. His fear was renewed. The finish line was so near, yet so far. The panic he experienced was all consuming.

His wife, Stephanie, appeared in the crowd ahead. She was happy and smiling, beckoning him on. There was David his son, dancing around, and little Molly laughing as she sat in her stroller. He tried desperately to reach them, but his legs felt leaden. His steps slowed. His family disappeared one by one.

Jonathan turned wildly, trying to find them in the crowd. It was no use; they were gone. Now the crowd began to disappear. Suddenly they all were all gone except his pursuer.

Renewed stress forced him to quicken his pace, and a sense of foreboding overwhelmed him anew. He could hear his pursuer's running feet. Jonathan, drenched with perspiration, tried even harder to run faster, but his legs would not obey. He was quickly becoming immobilized by terror.

His pursuer came closer and closer with unrelenting speed.

It was Miller, laughing maniacally. The laughter was loud, all around, echoing through Jonathan's brain. He held his head to stop the agonizing sound. At that moment he emitted a delirious scream of anguish. The horror had a hold on him. He fought the wet covers that clung to him, immobilizing him.

His pursuer was upon him, reaching for him. "No! No! No!" he shouted as he awakened from the nightmare.

With wakefulness, he felt relief. He sat up and tried to sort out his thoughts. After he overcome his initial confusion, Miller and Brown were all he could think about.

He thought, *I have to finish the job.* He concluded with finality, *Yes, finish the job.*

Jonathan's morose periods were lasting for longer and longer duration. He found it more difficult to raise himself out of the depressions. His safety was of no concern anymore. Lockhardt must die.

There was a sinking sensation in the pit of his stomach. *Miller does know'*, he thought. I *just finish the job soon.* "I must finish the job," he said aloud. "It can't end now; that's not the way it should be."

Anxiety was building dangerously as sweat oozed profusely from his skin. He gripped the mattress until his knuckles blanched white.

He uttered, "I'll make him pay!" His eyes cleared when he lay back and stared at the ceilin-. He used a corner of the sheet to mop the perspiration from his face and chest.

He slept late the next morning. \\'hen he awakened he felt desperately alone, abandoned. He had the need to touch or just be near people. He dressed hurriedly and ran out the door to jog in the nearby park.

The terrible loneliness stayed, although there were people around, walking or jogging. Little kids were playing.

There were older boys playing soccer. A ball rolled across Jonathan's feet as he walked along the path. He picked it up and gave it back to the child. The boy had the same happy, clear eyes as his son, David.

The boy smiled and said, "Thanks, mister," as he ran back to the game with his friends.

The Grotto was a relatively new restaurant, a converted warehouse at the edge of a very busy business district. It commanded a view of the city on one side, the bay and the marina on the other. It advertised the ultimate in dining and dancing.

Adam Lockhardt, with the ever-present air of omnipotence, mounted the broad stairs that led to the restaurant, for lunch. The lighting was subdued; not a sound could be heard.

He sat at the middle of the large dining room. He said, "Well, what do you recommend today, George?"

"Veal cutlets are special."

"No-just my usual."

"Will that be all, sir?"

"No, keep the martinis coming. I've had a long morning."

"Yes, sir," George said as he made his way through the other tables to the kitchen.

Adam decided after ordering to change his seat, to a quieter area near the window overlooking the street.

The Grotto was usually frequented by executives, white-collar workers and groups of well-dressed confidential secretaries with a smattering of blue-collar workers.

Adam gazed out over the city. He thought, my city, then suddenly something caught his eyes. It dawned on him that he had seen a white Mercedes several times in recent weeks. The realization had a disquieting effect on him. from his vantage point, he stared at the automobile.

The warning by Lieutenant Miller and that Detective Brown entered his mind. Miller had said, "The killer is murdering heavy drinkers, and your life may be in danger."

He looked again. The car was not occupied. But the vehicles he'd hit-with the woman and children in it - wasn't the car a white Mercedes?"

No, he thought. *It isn't possible. I must be imagining all this.* He downed his second martini.

After his fourth drink and a good lunch, he had regained some of his confidence, although the discomfort lurked in the recesses of his intoxicated mind. His last rational thought about the matter: Why would *Loring- want to follow me? Maybe the guy driving the white Mercedes just happened to be there.*

The martinis were helping him recapture the earlier feeling of omnipotence. After all, he was Adam Lockhardt. He was on top, and nothing could stop him. The doubts of a few moments ago were pushed to the back of his consciousness.

As he started out of the restaurant, there was that nagging little doubt that persisted. The thought only jarred his overblown confidence slightly, however.

Adam descended the stairs. At the bottom lie stopped to light a cigarette. Outside he climbed into his car. He checked the mirrorr; the white Mercedes' was gone. He smiled with a modicum of relief and thought, *Just my imagination.*

Jonathan had moved the Mercedes while Adam ate his lunch.

He had located a stool in the dimly lit liar, on the first floor, positioning himself to face both entrances. I could see Adam Lockhardt when he left the building.

Later he watched the executive descend the stairs, pause, light a cigarette, and leave the restaurant.

He looked at that well-groomed, hated face. Adam Lockhardt, financial tycoon schemer, drunk, manipulator, and above all, killer!

News Item-Society Page

Friday will mark the opening of a new exhibit. Paint mgs on consignment from the collection of Mr. and Mrs. Adam Lockhardt will be on display throughout the month of May.

The exhibit features the paintings of H. G. Wagner, well known for his realistic landscapes and street and harbor scenes. The collection can be seen in the yacht club's mt room, located in the marina.

Jonathan approached the hundred-year-old yacht club. He caught a whiff of the marina as he pushed through the decorative outer doors. He ordered his first drink and decided to gather as much information about Adam Lockhardt as he could. Drink in hand, he sauntered into the club's main ballroom to make small talk with the early arrivals.

Within a short period, the banquet room was filled to overflowing. The party was going full blast when he saw Lockhardt at the bar. Adam was speaking loudly to the group around him and to anyone who happened to pass within range of his voice.

Jonathan looked at that red face and listened to his abrasive voice as long as he could. He turned into the cocktail lounge and looked for a quiet table where he could regain his equilibrium.

His thoughts about his wife ranged from the first time he met her to the final death scene. The inner turmoil-and just remembering-created a deep depression. He nursed his drink a.good forty-five minutes before he could gather his inner resources and pull himself together.

The noises filtered through to his conscious mind, reminding him of the true purpose of attending this party.

In the ballroom, the party was still in full swing. On his way out, Jonathan noticed Adam Lockhardt leaning against a large plant. The moonlight shone on the pool of vomits. Adam's wife said, "Let Robert help you."

His slurred answer was not understandable. As Lockhardt passed out, the chauffeur caught him. Lie then maneuvered the unconscious man into the limousine.

Unknown to the Lockhardts, Jonathan followed when the car carrying the unconscious tycoon left the parking lot.

This editorial appeared in the morning paper:

Cities in four states are gripped in terror because of a serial-murder spree that has left drunken drivers dead in those states. The police are baffled.

Los Angeles Police Lieutenant Miller says, "It's the profile of a very disturbed man. We have consulted with a psychiatrist for advice.

"A great deal of police work is being done to catch the killer and I'm optimistic it will come to a successful conclusion."

But Los Angeles and other cities are on hair spring, ready to go off. The sale of hand guns has rocketed since the murders began.

The once-peaceful wealthy suburban areas have been plunged into a sickening nightmare of death and terror following the many unsolved killings in the past three years.

A Central Division police family has lost one Son to the so called "Extract Killer."

Timothy Houghton was one of the first to lose his life to the killer. His brother, Casey Houghten, says, "We're doing everything possible to help find the killer of my brother and the others."

Leading citizens have raised $400,000 as a reward for information leading to the killer or killers. "We're ready to fight," said the group's executive secretary, John Austin, "We are appalled and outraged by these murders."

The chain reaction to the murders is such that the victims may as well have been friends, as the entire community is involved in a common cause. "We're not advocating vigilante action, but we want to catch the killers."

Jonathan and Eleanor entered the banquet room at the Beverly Plaza. Notables from the political party in power at the time were present. Jonathan recognized influential businessmen and labor leaders. As the hours passed, the liquor intake increased considerably.

Eleanor had been raised in this atmosphere. She fitted in and appeared totally enraptured with the camaraderie.

Her chic, thin figure was adorned by a simple low-cut black lame' blouse, over an ankle-length skirt with a center slit that opened to just above the knee. She wore no jewelry and only a sparing amount of makeup. She had a new hairdo. There was an aura of subtle sensuality about her.

Jonathan smiled as he watched her move from one group of friends to another. She was self-assured; she was establishment.

The senator from California ended the evening. He spoke briefly about politicians and about his own accomplishments and goals. The applause died; the banquet was officially over.

Jonathan and Eleanor lay side by side in bed later. He stared at the ceiling, his hands cupped behind his head. He was deep in thought.

She watched him several minutes before speaking. Then she said softly,

"Penny."

"Huh?"

"Penny for your thoughts."

"They wouldn't be worth it."

He faced her and said blatantly, "I was just wondering where we are in our relationship, and where it will end."

"Must we be so serious?"

"Shouldn't we?" he asked.

"We understand one another; we have a good relation-ship. There's respect, and we trust each other."

"I've enjoyed the time we've spent together. We have a lot in common." His voice trailed off as he put his arms around her and gave her a hug.

She ran her fingers over his smooth, muscular back. A foghorn moaned in the distance. There was a crispness in the air that blew through the open bedroom window.

Eleanor experienced a feeling of puzzlement toward Jonathan. At times he posed a threat to her comfortable, unattached life; at other times he represented a need she hadn't known existed.

She quickly and decisively put the thought from her mind and gently started exploring his body with her fingers.

The momentum of their embrace escalated; their sharing of each other was fulfilling.

Later that evening, Jonathan was sitting in the white Mercedes, waiting for darkness. When it was time, he opened the door and climbed out, went around to the trunk, and collected the paraphernalia he needed. He moved in the shadows bordering the estate.

From his vantage point he had full view of the estate. He boldly cut across the vast lawn to the terrace door.

Jonathan peered through the windows that remained lit and saw the servants clearing the table after the dinner party. The going was easy; he had a clear view of the grounds and house.

He reached the library doors facing the formal gardens.

There he was: his victim. Jonathan paused for a moment and then walked through the conveniently open door. He moved quietly across the carpeted floor. The drunken industrialist lay sprawled on the leather couch. He aroused momentarily to stare briefly at Jonathan, made a grunting, guttural noise, folded his arms, and promptly fell asleep.

Jonathan, holding the syringe in his right hand, had reached the side of his quarry. He bent down and opened the stupefied man's shirt and plunged the needle into his exposed chest. Jonathan stood up, capped the syringe, and replaced it in its case. After the deed was done, he exited the way he had entered.

There was a flash of light. The security guard moved from windows to doors, making sure they were securely locked.

Jonathan, taking great care to keep from being seen, managed to get to the shadowed spot that bordered the lawn. Satisfied he had not been seen, he leaped over the six-foot wall, seemingly without effort.

He approached the corner of the fence and came face to face with another security guard, who stood only a feet away. He whirled and started toward his car. The guard said, "Hey, you. Wait a minute; I want to talk to you.

Jonathan had no choice. He rapidly ran deep into the shadows. The guard chased the intruder into the dense shrubbery. Jonathan, hearing shouts so near behind, turned, ready for the encounter.

A. small minority of a generation is relatively fearless; from this rank come some of our really great men. Unfortunately, we also get the not-so-great men, the type with the ability to hover on the brink of an abyss and yet keep their wits about them. They function coolly in the face of stress. Some of the fearless grow up to be heroes; then, there are others that end up as killers.

Jonathan casually turned toward the guard, who reached to grab him. Jonathan, seemingly without effort, sidestepped the man and administered a well-placed rabbit punch to the neck. The guard collapsed with a confused look on his face. In his car minutes later, Jonathan raced the motor and spun his wheels. The Mercedes leaped away from the curb and disappeared into the night.

Dr. Hunter came upon Miller in the bathroom, washing his hands. "Good morning, Hugh."

"Hi, Doc."

"Hugh, I've been thinking about our conversation of last week."

"Yeah, what about it?" Miller asked after he dried his hands and lit a cigarette. "Remember I said this man had a multi focal personality? I think in addition to obsessional preoccupation he could also be suffering from a depressive neurosis.

"Okay, I'll bite. Explain."

"It's a neurotic disorder in which long-lasting feelings of dejection arise in response to adverse external circumstances."

"And?"

"The precipitating stress may be sudden, caused by something such as bereavement, the breakdown of a relationship, or any kind of severe setback."

"Uh huh. That sounds reasonable."

"The relationship between the depression and the initial stress is clear, and the person, in a patient doctor relationship, may readily report it, although in some cases considerable (l uestioning may be needed. Depending on the nature of the stress, the depressive reaction may seem excessively severe or prolonged, as in this case of the killer."

"You're so right."

"In some cases patients are liable to be diagnosed as suffering from reactive depression; that can occur at any age. Even a resilient personality may be overcome by a depressive illness in the face of an overwhelming event, as in the death of a loved one." He paused to light his pipe. "In addition, neurotic depression differs from episodes of normal sadness in that the person cannot shake off the feelings of dejection. The affect is disproportionately intense and enduring. The depression may be as deep and lasting as an endogenous depression, but can be somewhat more varied. The depression tends to worsen in the evening."

"What can be done for him?"

"The outcome depends on the situation that provoked the illness, and the patient's recuperative resources. Resilient individuals tend to recover in time from serious setbacks or losses, while brittle personalities will tend to take longer to recover and are likely to relapse."

"If our killer had had treatment, would he still-kill?"

"That's hard to say. Most of these individuals can be helped by enhancing their ability to handle life's problems. A mildly disturbed patient whose concentration is not impaired may benefit by continuing at work."

"My suspect didn't do that, so can I assume he may be more than mildly disturbed?"

"It's possible, and as I said before, he is probably suffering from an overwhelming problem. He has to be caught soon." Hunter paused a moment before continuing. "I had a look at the autopsy' report, and this person is especially vicious and cunning, in addition to being intelligent."

"Thank you, Doc. This has given me some insight into this character's personality and maybe his problem, the poor bastard." Miller said as they prepared to leave the washroom.

Scott's wife greeted Jonathan effusively, with hugs and kisses. With a mock admonition, she asked, "Where have you been, and why didn't you call or write?"

Jonathan laughed happily and said, "Wait-wait a minute, Julie. I really have no defense, but would you accept a peace offering?"

Julie said playfully, "You devil, you always know how to get to me-by appealing to my avaricious nature." She gave him another big hug.

"I hope this pleases you," he said as he handed her a brightly wrapped gift.

"I have no doubt of that." As she carefully opened the package to reveal a gossamer black mantilla, she was momentarily speechless. Then she said, "Oh, Jonathan-it's lovely. I will have to wear this for a very special occasion. Thank you, love." She stood on tiptoes to kiss his cheek. She looked in his eyes a few seconds and continued to speak. "Now that you have vindicated yourself, I'll check on dinner," She turned and happily left the room with her gift.

Scott, wearing a smoking jacket. entered the room and led Jonathan into the dining room. Julie returned and they were seated.

For the next hour and a half, wine and dinner were served by the Swedish maid. The drinks were beginning,, to creep up on Jonathan. Each course served was better than the one before it, and they ate far too much.

He checked his watch: it was ten-thirty time had flown by. He hadn't realized the length of time they had spent over dinner.

Jonathan started his departure by apologizing for over staving, his welcome. Scott waved that away. saying that he always having him. Smiling, Julie and Scott walked to the door with Jonathan, who then said good-bye to his hosts..

Jonathan waited for Lockhardt. He was immaculate in a midnight blue suit and white on white shirt..

He stood with his back to the river. Before him passed a stream of people, moving slowly against a backdrop of buses and workers in cars impatient to get to their separate destinations. He watched their faces: women as well as men, smartly dressed, their heads held high as if for a photographer. He watched them closely as he waited for Lockhardt.

Finally he saw Adam taking his usual walk along the river to lunch. He was tall, goodlooking, expensively dressed, at ease. He walked as though he owned the world. He came closer to where Jonathan stood and looked squarely at Jonathan. Momentarily his steps became less certain; Adam was ill at ease in the spotlight of Jonathan's gaze. Lockhardt walked on. He thought, That man looked familiar. His lips clenched as he walked faster.

Jonathan followed, staying some distance behind. Lockhardt walked two blocks; then he crossed the boulevard and turning back to his office building. Jonathan stopped at the corner and watched him enter his office.

He muttered softly, "Your day is coming." He stood there a moment, then turned and retraced his steps back along the busy street.

On Saturday afternoon Adam Lockhardt and his wife attended a cocktail party. As usual, in a crowd he became the wheeler dealer as they wandered among the group's fashionably clothed men and women. Adam and Jonathan find themselves face to face. An air of uncertainty overcame Lockhardt as he looked into the other man's clear eyes. He paused a few seconds; there was an unearthly calm in that frozen moment. Time moved slowly, as if locked in a void. Lockhardt knew he had seen or met him before, but where? *I have to lay off the booze,* he thought. *Pay attention.* He smiled broadly and extended his hand. "I'm Adam Lockhardt, and this is my wife."

In a pleasant voice, Jonathan said, "This is Eleanor James, and I am Jonathan Loring."

"Have we met?"

Jonathan smiled. "I don't think so."

There was an uncomfortable pause. Adam asked, "What line of work are you in?"

"At present I'm between jobs," Jonathan answered as he sipped his cocktail.

Eleanor laughed. "Jonathan doesn't need to work."

Lockhardt felt uncomfortable, but why? He never lost control. He asked, "Do you live here?"

"At the moment."

"Will you be in town long."

"I haven't decided - why?"

"I'd like to invite you and Eleanor to a costume ball." Jonathan said, "We'll come. I can be reached at the marina, the *S.S.D.M*" Jonathan's persuasive smile allowed Adam to relax as he departed to the nearest bar. Loring forgotten, he said to an old friend, "Jim, what ever happened to Justin?"

"You know, I haven't seen him since New York," Jim answered.

CHAPTER XI

Raymond Keystone opened the discussion on the Sunday morning "Roundtable." "Ladies and Gentlemen, may I present to you Dr. Hunter, psychiatric consultant to Central Division P.D., Dr. Jerrell Becker, chief of psychiatry, Donner Medical Center. Also, Dr. Russell Tineculas, State Board of Psychiatry." Turning to face the assembled group, Key-stone said, "Gentlemen, I'm sure we are all acquainted with the recent rash of murders covering four states, and we are here today to discuss the type of personality that could create this type of crime wave. In the process, we will examine the causative factors that could send him or her on a murder spree. I will ask each of you to make a brief opening state ment." He paused. "Dr. Hunter, we will begin with you because you have been closely associated with the case in question."

"Thank you, Raymond. I believe we are dealing with a multifaceted personality, one who is cunning, shrewd, and intelligent," said Dr. Hunter. "He is being driven by rage to excessive and irrational acts of violence. It appears obvious to me, and I'm sure my learned colleagues will agree, that he has a grudge against heavy drinkers or drunks."

"Why is that, Doctor?"

Hunter replied, "Quite possibly a drunk has done harm to him or someone he loves."

"Dr. Becker, your statement."

"I agree," Becker said. "We are confronted with a complex personality driven to acts of violence through a state of violent anger. He is quite possibly suffering some form of fanaticism; this is suggested by the intensity of his violence. The killer does not seem to be responding with reason, because the murders are irrational. I've read the various reports and there seems to be a fugue state."

"What's a fugue state?"

"You understand, we cannot make a diagnosis because we have not had the chance to examine him as a patient. We can only surmise on the manifested irrational behavior. To get to your question: a fugue state is a transitory, abnormal behavior patterns marked by aimless wandering and sonic alteration of consciousness. It is usually, but not always, followed by amnesia. I believe the killer is always in possession of himself."

"Thank you, Dr. Becker. Dr. Russell Tineculas, whose expertise in abnormal psychology is world renowned. Doctor."

"Thank you, Raymond. I think we are dealing with a group of neuroses characterized by recurrent thoughts, feeling, or impulses, known as obsessions, along with repetitive acts, or 'compulsions,' and that the person may recognize his acts as morbid. He may feel a strong inner resistance, but is unable to stop. These people are excessively fastidious. careful in all details. They have a loathing for disorder, and I must point out that an obsessional preoccupation may be controlled and/or limited for several years before the full-fledged illness begins, probably triggered by some incident either large or sniall, as in the death of a loved one, or dear friend."

"You think the killer's illness actually existed for some time and only in the last three years manifested itself?" Raymond asked.

"Yes, it's possible-and the precipitating stress possibly entails a clash between the patient's moral standard and his normal impulses following some evocative experience."

Dr. Becker said, "I agree with Russell to a point: obsessive rituals usually include repetitive acts and procedures as well as thoughts. But, as we all know, they may vary greatly in different patients."

"Are you saying violence and death are other characteristic sources of preoccupation?" Raymond asked.

"In essence that may be true," Hunter said, "but I think the killer has experienced a shocking and unacceptable situation that is too painful to remember; the causative factor is then retained only in the subconscious mind. As we all know, the technical term for this is repression.

"It was pointed out a short while ago that the killer was possibly in possession of himself at all times," Raymond said.

"That may or may not be true, Raymond. We are dealing with a lonely person and are only seeing his overt acts of violence. Until the killer is caught we can only deal in suspicion."

"I understand," Raymond said. "Would either one or all of you please elaborate on repression?"

"Repression," Dr. Hunter said, "is a defense mechanism whereby a person unconsciously banishes unacceptable ideas, feelings or, impulses from the consciousness, but this is only a textbook definition." Hunter paused and then continued...A person using repression to obtain relief from mental conflict is unaware that he is forgetting unpleasant situations as a way of avoiding them. I feel that the killer is not experiencing repression. He is fu]]y aware of what he is doing, and after reading the autopsy report, I feel we are dealing with a homicidal personality who is cunning and intelligent. The methods used point to intelligence."

"It's as you stated earlier," Dr. Becker said. "This is a multifocal personality. If this person suffered a loss-for example, of a loved one-we could be dealing with a depressed person. Situational or reactive depression. In the younger person it is generally not as severe as in an adult, and the effect may be devastating when it breaks up a young family."

Hunter said, "A point well taken. If a marriage achieves a reasonably happy balance, intrusion into or disruption of that union could upset the balance, as in the death, say, of the wife and children. The person may resent a lack of understanding in others, but in his depressed state he is far from being Mr..Warmth himself. He may appear aloof or indifferent."

Becker said, "We all understand that depression involves unrecognized and unacceptable anger, but you've said the killer is aware of his actions. That gives us another perspective."

"Gentlemen," Raymond Key-stone said, "you have been very helpful, but we are running out of time. We will not be able to resolve the problem, but we have thirty seconds to quickly summarize. Dr. Hunter, would you begin, since you re closer to the situation?"

Dr. Hunter said, "We are dealing with a multifocal personality-who is intelligent, shrewd, and has over the past month shown cunning as well. The man or woman has had a loss-quite possibly of a loved one-and is killing because of the towering rage."

"I feel," said Dr. Becker, "the killer has experienced a shocking and unacceptable situation. There is a feeling of intense anger due to a loved one's being killed or maimed by a heavy drinker, and he wasn't present to help in some way.

I agree he is being driven by rage to excessive and irrational acts of violence." Dr. Tineculas said, "My colleagues have covered the situation well."

Keystone said, "Thank you, Drs. Becker, Hunter, and Tineculas." Then he turned to the TV camera. "That's all we have time for today. In our next program we will have an in depth study of the Save the Seals program. This is Raymond Keystone bidding yon adieu until next Sunday, when we will present another Sunday morning 'Roundtable.'

Jonathan slipped quietly through the partially open doors. He stood for a moment surveying the room and the man passed out on his couch. He advanced surreptitiously into the room. As he came near the man, Jonathan realized to his surprise that the man's eyes were open and that he had been watching him as he walked to the couch.

In a slurred voice the man asked, "Who are you, and what are you doing in my house?"

Jonathan hesitated. The question had caught him off guard, but the emotion he felt was so powerful that he was beyond caring.

He said with a laugh, "You people are not usually awake." He removed the carrying case from an inner pocket. "We will soon remedy that."

"Who are you? What are you doing? You're that killer." He attempted to struggle into a sitting position. "I'll call the police!"

Jonathan in one easy motion pushed him back into a prone position. The victim struggled drunkenly and tried to yell for help, the call was barely heard in the room.

Jonathan said, "I don't think you'll be needing any more to drink. Why don't I just see to that night now." Skillfully he pressed a sensitive area on the drunken man's neck, rendering him unconscious.

He withdrew the needle, put it back in its case, and started out of the room. He turned at the doorway for one last look. He glowered at the man on the couch, who struggled to sit up and rolled off onto the carpeted floor. The news clipping fluttered to the floor.

Just before the cocktail hour, the executive worked at a measured pace in his carpeted office on the twentieth floor. He worked on a merger that would unite the two top corporations in the country.

He had started his company fifteen years ago on a shoestring. He had been hard driving, hard drinking, and successful. His business climbed meteorically over the years, and when this merger he was developing came to fruition, the possibilities would be limitless.

He glanced at his watch-nearly 7:00 p.m..-and took a sip of the drink at his elbow. He phoned his wife. "I'll be leaving in the next half hour."

"Hurry home, darling. We still have sonic packing to do."

"I forgot that," he said. "I'll just tie up a few loose ends and be on my way. See you soon, dear." He hung up the receiver. The silence was broken by a shuffling sound. He sipped his drink and yelled, "Who's there?"

There was no reply; the quiet was complete. He thought, His *ears are playing tricks on 'lie.*

The long weekend ahead would help get him in just the right frame of mind for his meeting next week. He stood up and took a large swallow from his "lass. He scratched his backside as he stared out the window at the lengthening shadows in the street below. After a few minutes he put his papers away, shrugged into his coat, and left his office.

He had advanced a few steps into the outer office when everything went black. He had been hit from l)ehind; his body sank to the floor, stunned. The fallen executive rolled over on his back and through the clearing haze saw his attacker. He said, "Who are you? Get out of here'."

His assailant gave him a malevolent stare as he injected the lethal substance into the cardiac space.

The victim exclaimed,. "What have you done?" as he felt the numbness creep rapidly throughout his body. Lie tried to lift his hands to strike out, but there was no coordination. He could only stare helplessly at his attacker, who slowly pushed him back, pressing the news clipping into his pocket.

Jonathan didn't wait for the victim's last moments. He slipped out the door as the 6rst waves of seizures gripped the man on the floor. Before he died, his mouth felt dry, as his tongue swelled, shutting off the remaining air, suffocating the floundering man.

Later, Jonathan sat in the privacy of his bedroom, contemplating his recent action. He thought, *They deserve to die for all the hurt and pain they cause. That kind never learns!*

He winced when he thought of his dead family. As he caressed the photograph of the family, he thought, *Society should thank me for what I did. I am trying to show the',, the way. l will have to get rid of them all.*

Jonathan felt at that moment that he had to rid society of drinking problems. He took a deep breath and smiled.

CHAPTER XII

It was evening. Miller sat in his office. The inevitable cigarette smoldered in the overflowing ashtray as he read the evening news.

JUDGE DEERBORNE MURDERED

The City of Los Angeles was stunned by the murder of Judge Deerborne. "This is a very serious problem for our area," said the police commissioner.

When asked about the note that was attached to the judge's body and the odor that filled the room, the commissioner declined to answer.

A source, who prefers to remain unknown, stated, "The note said that Judge Deerborne had been accused by his killer of releasing excessive drukers with light sentences." The source also said that the judge lived long enough to make a statement, althoua~h he was unable to identify his killer.

The judge was hit from behind as he walked through his parking garage. The assailant, a male, came from a shadowed area and said in a whisper, "You will never release another alcoholic."

The police task force had doubled its efforts to find the killer. The force includes representatives of both the police and private sector of law enforcement.

Miller slammed the newspaper down on the desk and said, "Damn, when will this stop! Now he's killed the goddamn judge!"

In the captain's office fifteen minutes later, Miller said, "I know my theory has been received rather lightly, but I'm convinced I'm right."

"You mean you still think this Loring is the killer?" the captain asked.

"Yes - I do.

"Why him? We still have over seventy-five people to check!"

"You won't find anything, "Miller said with frustration in his voice. He lit a cigarette. "When you get an idea in your head, you hold on tenaciously."

"I know I'm right!"

"Where's your proof?"

"I don't have proof, but I'll get it. I don't know where; I'll get it."

"Okay, Hugh, you show me proof. Just find me something other than a gut feeling!" Miller interrupted rudely, "Let's look at the facts. Fact one: Loring's family was killed."

"So were a lot of others' relatives. Loring is a responsible man. I think you're wrong."

"Fact two: The killings stayed shortly after he left that cabin in Montana."

"Hugh, let go. Please!"

"Fact three: he has knowledge of chemistry and anatomy, and he had the time to develop his extract while he was in Montana."

"Did you find anything there? Chemicals, labels, anything to supoport fact three?"

"Hugh, you cannot arbitrarily accuse someone on your gut feeling."

"Fact four: Loring is athletic. He frequents skiing events. He has traveled to most of these places. He is a music buff. A tall, slender man has been present at the time of most of the killings."

"So? That's not proof."

"Too many coincidences for comfort, and I believe Loring is here to kill Lockhardt."

"Hugh, we've gone through all this. That is beyond all logic. The man has been killing only recent alcoholics. Be-sides, why didn't he kill Lockhardt a long time ago?"

"How would I know how a nut's mind works? \\'ho knows what set him off? The man is not stable. Dr. Gordon made that comment in passing only once, and it has stuck in my mind ever since." He paused and then continued. "He knows he's being followed and on two occasions has led my men all over. Now, if he wasn't guilty, why would he do that?"

The captain said, with raised hands, "Okay, okay, laugh. Keep digging and bring me something concrete!"

"All right, I will!" Hugh said, and he lit a cigarette from the other cigarette butt as he left the captain's office."

Jonathan dreamed of his early childhood. \\'hat fun he had had on the summer vacations. At the end of the school year he dreamed of the important things that he had done during summer break. The plunges into the nearby river, hiking with his dad, the beach, and the baseball games with the boys.

He felt good when he dreamed of baseball; he was proud of his games.

He was a good pitcher as well as a good batter.

His mood changed abruptly when the next dream flashed through his mind. He broke into a cold sweat.

He was back in his old neighborhood. A frightening occurrence. His heart pumped hard; the strangeness was overwhelming. He ran home to his mother, who would know what was wrong and make it all right. He ran down street after street; everything was distorted.

Jonathan as a boy. He ran up the front steps to his house. He banged his small fists against the front door. He shouted, "Mommy, Mommy, open the door! It's me, let me in.

Hysteria gripped him now. He rang the bell, shouted, and pounded and kicked the door. He slumped to his knees, exhausted and whimpering. Sweat poured from his forehead and into his eyes. He wiped it away with a small hand.

The door opened as if by magic. He ran hopefully into the front hall and raced through the rooms downstairs hoping to find his mother. He burst through the kitchen door. When he didn't find her, he tore out of the kitchen and up the stairs two steps at a time, falling a couple of times.

The distance between the stairs and his mother's bedroom seemed miles long. Panic stricken, he shouted, "Mom! Mom"' Jonathan flung open the bedroom door expecting to see his mother taking a nap. The little boy flipped the light switch, but there was no light. Terrified, he ran to the vacant bed. He hid his face in the bedspread and sobbed until be could cry no more. Finally he got a hold on himself.

Minutes went by before he was brave enough to dry his eyes and look around the familiar room.

His eyes fell upon the high-back chair. He quietly approached it and stepped cautiously around to face the occupant. The boy's anxiety returned when he saw the person was not his mother.

The stranger rose and took a step toward the frightened child. The boy's gaze was fixed trancelike on the stranser, who was dressed in a black suit.

The stranger spoke. "Hello, Jonathan. I am your uncle. I have come to take you home with me."

The horror of the statement forced the boy to back away. He shouted repeatedly, "No! No! I won't! I won't! I want to stay here and wait for my mother and dad. I don't know you."

The man started to I au"~h hysterically, and his face changed. It was Lockhardt. Jonathan awakened with a start, drenched with sweat.

Eleanor and Jonathan were dressing in their homes. She toweled herself after stepping from a long, luxurious bath.

She thought of Jonathan, who never made demands, and was not sure of her feelings about him. She now realized that from the beginning of their relationship, he had guided her ever so gently. It had been so easy to be with him, and she had not been aware of the sublety of his technique as he was directing her.

He was a good sport, went along with her and her friends. Eleanor was not sure, but at times he seemed more aloof than at other times, and there were evenings when they were out when it seemed he made an extra effort to get through the evening.

She never knew how he really felt about their relationship. There was always that distant quality. She was chilled when she thought of that. Their associate on was at that point now. She was not sure how to respond.

She wriggled into her costume for the J)all and thought, *I won't force the issue tonight.* It might be nice if she could have him always. She smiled at this.

Jonathan dressed as John Standish. He dressed meticulously in his costume of white ruffled-front shirt and pale-gray suit. He viewed himself in the mirror as he fastened the jacket. As he put on his wig he thought about how easily, one could change his appearance. The pressures and anxieties that had been hidden were building within him.

Jonathan added the finishing touches to his costume. He was not sure what the evening would bring, but he would concentrate on the important night ahead.

Subconsciously he had become uneasy about his and Eleanor's relationship. It was not always easy for him to handle fun and games, especially with the tremendous task ahead. Neither had made demands, but he felt there would be if the relationship continued. He had to face the fact that most women wanted to be loved regardless of what they say. A lasting love was built on consideration of the two involved.

Obviously women's lib had not completely erased that.

Jonathan thought, *Enough of this*, as he concentrated on the night ahead and Adam Lockhardt. He took one last look around before leaving.

He climbed into the limousine and wondered if he would be followed this evening. Sure enough, after a block he spotted his tail, only the color of the car had changed. By the time he arrived at Eleanor's, he had decided how to dispose of Adam Lockhardt, in spite of his tail. Jonathan knew essentially how the evening would end: Adam Lockhardt would pass out and the job could be done.

In reply to his ring, Eleanor opened her door. She was regally clad in her costume. In one white gloved hand she held a fan, while the other daintily lifted the full-hooped skill as she curtsied. She was lovely. Her gown was a deep green, with a plunging neckline, and jewels sparkled at her throat. Her ensemble complemented her auburn hair.

He folded her hand over his arm and escorted her out of the apartment building to the open door of the limousine. He smiled as he assisted her into the car. He said, softly, "You are especially beautiful tonight."

"*Merci*, monsieur," she sighed happily as they were driven away. The sky was black velvet with a sprinklings of stars that shone like diamonds.

"You are-magnificent. You'll be the belle of the ball," he said as they faced each other.

She squeezed his hand and answered happily, "Well, let's get this show on the road." They both laughed.

The limousine stopped before the well4it mansion to allow Jonathan and Eleanor to get out.

Somewhere along the way they had picked up Scott and Julie. They climbed out of the car and entered the decorative double doors, passing a footman on either side. Inside was an atmosphere of gaiety.

Each couple was announced with the pomp of years gone by. The Lockhardts greeted each couple within the main ball-room, which had seventeenth-century decor. Adam Lockhardt laughed loudly, kissed some of the women on the cheeks, and slapped the husbands on the back while his wife stood graciously by, smiling, well coifed, and wearing the costume of a southern belle. Adam was Rhett Butler.

Jonathan, before his turn in line, said, "I feel like a Pilgrim who has finally arrived."

"This is really a fancy get together," Eleanor said from behind her fan.

"flow are you, ol' man?" Lockhardt asked.

"Great, and thanks for the invitation," Jonathan answered.

"Good to have you."

Mrs. Lockhardt said to them both, "Enjoy yourself."

Adam's happiness was genuine, inspired l)y the fact that this ball and his life were total successes.

The waiters and footmen were dressed in similar seventeenth-century costumes. They wandered among the guests with trays of drinks and succulent tidbits.

Jonathan escorted Eleanor into the crowded ballroom, with Scott and Julie bringing up the rear. Scott and Julie spotted old friends and the couples parted.

Mrs. Lockhardt appeared in the doorway. She was radiant. One could not tell if the "glow was from happiness o)r the liquid refreshment she had consumed-or both.

Eleanor said to her, "I am impressed. Congratulations on your successful gathering."

"Thank you," Mrs. Lockhardt said.

Adam went straight to the bar. \\'hen all the guests had arrived, he said, "I'm glad that's over. Give me my usual and make it a double."

The drink was placed before him; he drank it right away. "Give me another." He took his second drink and joined the crowd. He yelled, "Hey, Doug," and disappeared.

Jonathan and Eleanor danced and wandered throughout the great hall, avoiding bumping into the other costumed guests.

Dinner was announced. Jonathan folded Eleanor's hand over his extended elbow and escorted her into the dining room, where the chandeliers sparkled like diamonds near the ceiling. They located their places. A footman pulled out the chairs for them to be seated.

Jonathan said to Eleanor, "I'm famished."

She said, "Ditto here. I thought we would never eat."

"Those little sandwiches don't do it."

Scott and Julie were seated across from them. Julie asked, "Can you believe this party?"

"It's no(a party, honey; it's a costume ball," Scott said smiling.

"Oh, there was a peasant or two in my past. To me it's still a party."

"And a big one," Eleanor remarked.

They all laughed.

Soup was served, and course after course followed with the appropriate wines.

During dinner, Jonathan noticed that Adam was (1 uite drunk. He had watched him surreptitiously.

Lockhardt was in his glory, conducting an animated conversation with the guests nearest him.

Eleanor turned to Jonathan. She was disturbed by the strange smile on his face. She had seen him off guard, staring at Adam Lockhardt. She turned quickly away.

Later, Jonathan danced with Julie and Scott with Eleanor..

Jonathan said to Julie, "\Well, squirt, I didn't tell you earlier, but you are beautiful."

"You're not so bad yourself," Julie said. "I didn't remember how handsome you were.

"My, my. You'll have me blushing in a minute," he said as he whirled her around the floor.

Eleanor said to Scott, "Have you known Jonathan long?"

"Yes-since he and Stephanie were married. He's a good man , had a lot of problems."

"I know. He seems to have coped well with it." The dance ended at that moment.

Eleanor and Jonathan danced the last dance of the eve-fling. She was relieved to see he was himself again. She thought she had been mistaken at dinner.

Eleanor entered the living room carrying a tray with coffee and two cups. Jonathan, his jacket open, was sitting comfortably on the low, ultra-modern couch. He said, "This was some evening."

"You're right ," she said as she set the tray down. "Here, let me help you."

"Oh, no, this is simple. I'm fine." She filled two cups and passed one to him. She slipped her feet out of her shoes and sat down on the couch beside him.

He pressed the switch on the stereo and the tone arm slowly dipped and touched the rim of the spinning disc. The first notes of Beethoven filled the room. He said, "The right lighting, the right music, and. best of all, the right woman. The end to a perfect evening."

She smiled as she leaned her head hack on the couch. They both relaxed as the music played on. Later, Jonathan kissed her good night as he left for home.

He waited as the doorman opened the door. "Good night, Mr. Loring," the doorman said. "Good night."

The limousine had driven him the short distance to his apartment, the nondescript car following some distance behind.

Earlier, the lieutenant had watched as the limousine pulled away with Jonathan and his friends. He had followed them at a safe distance, and watched as the man and woman alighted and entered their home.

He had brought the radio transmitter to the side of his face, pressed down the transmission switch, and said, "Car One to Mobile Unit Two. Come in, Sidney."

The voice had come back slightly cracked. "Car Two here. What's happening, Lieutenant?"

"Subject is just entering the James apartment building. The Limo is waiting, so it won't be long.
Where are you?"

"Outside the Lockhardt residence, across the street."

"Okay, stay there."

Thirty minutes later, Jonathan came out of Eleanor's building and climbed into the limousine. Miller followed at a distance; he watched as Jonathan entered his apartment minutes later.

Miller settled down to wait, very miserable without his cigarettes. He rummaged around in the glove compartment and finally found an old, crushed pack with two flattened cigarettes. He said, "Anything in a pinch," as he carefully lit his first cigarette in an hour. He didn't have to wait long and was surprised by his quarry's sudden appearance.

He said into the transmitter, "Sidney.' I think our man is making a move." He paused. "Yep, there he goes. He's driving a white Mercedes, California number XZY 910. I'll get back to you; I'm moving. Get some backup." Miller had parked some distance away in a shadowed area.

Jonathan, dressed in black, walked surreptitiously into the underground garage to his apartment building. He made sure the street was clear before he drove out. He thought that Miller was too smart and had made some kind of discovery. Jonathan wondered, what *does he know, or think he knows? But I can't risk Lockhardt's getting away. Swift action is what it takes now, and tonight is the night.*

Jonathan had to calm himself. He breathed deeply to allow his tense abdominal muscles to relax. His heart slowed when his breathing was back to normal. He checked the rear-view mirror, and there it was the same car following a block behind.

He drove around for a few minutes; the car stayed with him. Jonathan drove to an all-night cafe', parked, and went in. He continued through to the men's room, where he climbed out a rear window into an alley that led to a darned street where he had another car.

As he drove out of the city, he experienced a sense of anticipatory euphoria.

Miller waited outside for ten minutes before going inside. He opened the door and walked all the way through the cafe'. No Loring. He felt panic for a moment as he searched through the empty booths to discover the open window above one of the lavatory stalls.

He ran out the front and jumped into his car. He shouted into the transmitter, "I've lost him. The bastard climbed out of a caf6 window. He probably has another car. Get that backup now. It's going down now'.""

Jonathan had checked the leather kit that contained the lethal dose of extract, enough to put Lockhardt to sleep permanently.

His rage had pushed him into action on this night. He brought the car to a stop in the shadows of the tall shrubbe1y' and surveyed the area. He slowly climbed out of the driver's seat. He quietly and quickly moved from shadow to shadow as he ran to the wall surrounding the Lockhardts' estate. With the ease of an athlete he scaled the wall and dropped catlike to the grounds inside.

His anger had not abated as he raced through the grounds to the guest house where he had last seen Lockhardt. As he gulped in air, he felt the blood pounding in his ears.

He opened the door to the house and determined that his quarry was still asleep. As he walked over to the prone figure, logic struggled to take hold, but the compulsion to rid the world of this drunken sot was too strong. He shook Adam roughly to awaken him.

Jonathan wore gloves. He sat looking at the huddled figure of Lockhardt, whose eyes stared 'vacantly across the room. Adam's hand hung limply between his knees.

On the table beside Jonathan lay the small box, with the syringe already primed.

A low, guttural noise escaped Lockhardt's throat. His eyes began to focus as he came out of his whiskey stupor.

Jonathan began to speak in a flat, unemotional tone, never taking his eyes off Adam's pale face.

There were moments during his recital when anger welled to the surface, along with the loathing he felt for the man before him. He described the feelings he had when he was told of his family's deaths, how he felt when Adam the drunk had walked away without a scratch.

He spoke of his contempt for the judge who gave hini a veritable slap on the wrist. He told Adam how he had followed the Lockhardt family in the news: the new cars, furs for his wife for every event, his defiance of the law, his backslapping and ego-preening in public. Jonathan enumerated these things in a cold and bitter 'voice. He pointed out that Adam's family had everything on a silver platter while his own had been destroyed by Adam's drunkenness.

The horror of the narration finally reached Lockhardt. It sickened him. He emitted another throaty animal moan, the sound of profound anguish.

Then he realized that Loring intended to kill him. He looked around like a caged animal, searching for a way out. But Loring could easily Stop any escape attempt he could make.

Adam finally said, "They'll catch you -"his voice trailed off.

"Maybe, but do you realize how many people out there don't care if you die? More than fifty percent." Jonathan paused and then asked, "How are they going to catch me? Witnesses? There are none. Motive? Why didn't I do this sooner? Fingerprints?" Jonathan held his gloved hands up for Adam to see. "Why should anyone suspect me? The killings have been of men involved in recent incidents." He smiled when he saw the helpless look on Adam's face. He continued. "I knew you wouldn't remember me. I wasn't in the courtroom when you received your slap on the wrist. I watched yon on TV. I saw your loathsome, "grinning face when you stopped outside the court to spew your platitudes." He stopped momentarily to look at the miserable expression on Adam's face. Then he asked, "How long did it take you to start drinking again? A day? Two days?"

Adam said, with desperation in his voice, "Please-please. I can't-I can make it up to you-I have money, friends who will help you.

Jonathan laughed mockingly. He waited a moment before answering, "I have money. You're too late to offer help. Can you replace my family? The years I've lost? The anguish? Did you ever think of the hell you might have caused? I doubt it; you never rave it a second thought."

"Please-"

"What am I suppose to do, Lockhardt? Let you go on living? No, your time bas come." with that, he stood, removed the prefilled syringe, and applied the large-bore needle.

Adam made a drunken lurch to ret away, but Jonathan easily pushed him back on the couch. Adam cowered. His hands were held up as if to shield himself. He said, "Please! Please!" as he began to sob. His movements were feeble and ineffective as he stumbled drunkenly off the couch in another attempt to cross the room toward the side door.

Miller tried repeatedly to reach Sidney.

"Car One to Car Two. Where the hell are you, Sidney.'"

"We're in back of the estate." He eased his thumb off the switch, holding the transmitter near his face. Then he said, "We've found a car parked in back. I think he's in-side."

"Well, get in there!" Miller shouted.

The police radio crackled as Stampley said to Miller, "We've found it, the evidence, in a storage bin on Loring's yacht. A journal of news clippings covering the death of his family, the first murders in Aspen. All up to date."

"Did you hear that, Sidney? Go get him, move!" Miller shouted. "I'm on my way. E.T.A. two minutes."

A voice crackle back, "We're going in the front, Lieutenant." A second voice said, "All set at the east gate. Going in now!"

Sidney spoke quietly into his hand unit. "He's in the first guest house." He lowered his hand unit, clicked it off, and stuffed it into his pocket as he walked around the large pool toward the guest house.

Casey came around front. His gun in one hand, he walked catlike along the steps to the patio. off to the side other officers were moving in fast.

Miller screeched to a stop and ran toward the policemen surrounding the cottage. He could feel the hand unit as it bumped his side. He didn't turn his head to look when Sidney said, "You were right all along."

Miller said, "Why the hell didn't he leave my town? The poor bastard."

Sidney strode ahead, up the broad walk. Lie asked, "Are you coming, Lieutenant?"

"No, you go on," Miller said. "Get in there. Lie's all yours.

Jonathan had blocked Adam's exit in two easy strides and had shoved him into the nearest chair. Lie pressed the carotid arteries on either side of Adam's throat and then plunged the needle into the unconscious man's chest. He was injecting the deadly liquid into his heart as Sidney burst through the door.

"Hold it, don't move!" Sidney shouted.

Lockhardt's heart pumped furiously, carrying the lethal fluid throughout his body within six-tenths of a second.

Sidney yelled, "Call an ambulance!" to an officer outside.

Jonathan said, "You're too late. If he lives he will never wheel and deal again." Then he made a foolish move. He attempted to escape out the patio side door, where he grappled with Casey and was shot.

Sidney came out and said, "We were too late. Christ, he had injected the stuff. The needle was still in the ray's chest."

"Did you call an ambulance?" Miller asked.

"Yes, two ambulances. Lockhardt is dead now. He had already passed out. I don't think he felt anything. Loring tried to ret away and was shot in the shoulder."

Miller watched as the first ambulance drove out of the grounds, followed by the squad cars.

Miller said to Jonathan, as the latter was wheeled from the guest house, "Why? You could have gone anywhere. You could have gotten the hell out of my town.

Jonathan stared at Miller for a long moment and answered, "You had your job to do; I had a job to do. He had to die, just as my family died." The attendants lifted him into the waiting ambulance. *Christ almighty, I need a cigarette*, Miller thought.

As he was going through the open door, Jonathan asked, "What gave me away?"

"Mostly a gut feeling on my part," Miller replied.

Jonathan laughed. "Caught on a hunch. Well, I guess it was a matter of time, but why me? There must have been hundreds who felt the same as I."

Miller said, "There was more than a gut feeling. It was your background. The description of a tall, well-dressed man on more than one occasion fitted you generally. There were other bits of information. And the timing was right." With that, he waved the ambulance on. Miller's steps were slow as he followed behind. *I have to have a cigarette*, he thought.

Jonathan was committed to Lyons Psychiatric Institution for evaluation. He was in a deeply depressed state.

EPILOGUE

Six weeks after Jonathan's commitment this story appeared on KISG TV News:

EXTRAT KILLLR ESCAPES

Jonathan Loring escaped from Lyons Psychiatric Institution Tuesday evening. It is believed that Loring walked away from the hospital dressed in one of the doctors' laboratory coats. Loring was committed six weeks ago after a murder spree in the affluent communities in four states. Police have been alerted throughout California and surrounding states to be on the lookout for him.

Loring smiled as he crossed the state line into New Mexico. The smart doctors and nurses never noticed the patients, especially' if they were deeply depressed and never caused trouble.

ABOUT THE AUTHOR

Born in a small town in the Midwest, I. S. Grant holds a degree in nursing from Pasadena City College. She says, "As a nurse, I have seen the tragic end products of drunkenness: death of the innocent, family suffering, mutilation of bodies." She hopes Walking a Thai Line will enhance public awareness regarding this growing problem.

Ms. Grant is the mother of four children:

Eric, Robert, Kelly Ann, and Russell. Her interests include reading, writing, and travel.